After Midnight

Angela Warren

Contents

Chapter 1

The airport was one of the best places to people watch.

There were families with cranky kids and moody teenagers, overexcited travelers, anxious flyers trying to calm their nerves before boarding, and those who were clearly hungover as they sat hunched over in sweats while nursing both a coffee and water.

Then there were people like me who were traveling alone and simply going through the motions.

Having flown out to San Francisco to be with my family for the holidays—which had been exactly the break I needed after not being back on the west coast for almost two years—I'd arrived at the airport a few hours before my flight home to give myself time to get through security, grab some food, and relax at my gate. Something I was now regretting, as my flight back to Boston had been delayed. It was going on the fifth hour I'd been sitting in an uncomfortable chair and I'd already run through the episodes I'd downloaded of Netflix's latest hit.

Hence the people watching.

With my headphones in—void of any music in an attempt to salvage what was left of my phone battery—and a lukewarm coffee in my hands, I let my attention wander.

I could hear the man who sat behind me having much too loud of a conversation on the phone, with someone I assumed to be a colleague, about his newest business venture. Words like investment, capital, and shareholders had me tuning out while also making me proud on some level this stranger was working so hard to get an idea off the ground.

Then there was the woman sitting beside me who, despite having to be at least double my age, didn't try to hide the fact that she was sexting someone named Jimmy. Something I wish I'd never had to see as I quickly averted my gaze from the extra large font on her screen.

Except doing so had me momentarily eyeing a couple at the end of the aisle, likely a few years younger than me, who were sharing a seat and making out like they were in the privacy of a bedroom and not surrounded by strangers.

But, I mean, if that made the time pass faster, all the power to them.

Feeling the awkwardness of watching another couple get it on wash over me, coupled on top of the slight prick of envy in my chest, I turned my head and tuned in to the conversation between the parents two rows ahead of me and their young children.

"But why do we have to wait so long?" the older of the two kids asked, looking to be around eight years old as he sat on the carpeted floor.

"Yeah, it's sunny outside. Why are they saying there's a storm?" the younger one pressed.

Which, to be fair, were valid questions for kids their age. Before either of their parents could answer, however, a voice crackled on the overhead speaker.

"Attention passengers aboard Flight 534 to Boston." A hush settled over the waiting area as everyone listened to the announcement, hoping we were finally able to board. "The flight's departure time has been pushed back to 7:00pm. Boarding will take place thirty minutes before, so please have your ticket ready at that time. Thank you."

A collective groan filled the area. This was the third delay announcement in two hours, all because of a freak snowstorm sweeping over the middle of the country. And while I understood the safety precautions the airline had to take, I almost wished they'd just cancel the flight and put me, as well as everyone else, out of our misery.

Trying to look on the bright side though, the extra delay gave me the push I needed to abandon my seat and track down some semblance of a dinner, knowing I wouldn't be eating on the flight any time soon. My stomach grumbled for what felt like the hundredth time as I stood, grabbed my carry-on, and subtly nodded to a woman who had been leaning against the wall for the last hour that she could take my seat before heading towards the dining hall.

Thirty minutes later, after I'd demolished a cheeseburger and fries, I had my gaze locked on my phone as I swiveled around on the bar stool to hop down, only to stumble into another person who'd been walking past.

A person who was clearly male and definitely in shape if the strong chest muscles beneath my palms were anything to go by.

"Shit, sorry. My bad," I said, righting myself as the stranger's hands fell from around my waist.

Looking up at him with a red hue of embarrassment coating my cheeks, I immediately noticed the way his lips twisted upward and laughter filled his dark brown eyes. "Don't worry about it," he replied.

Knowing there was nothing else for me to say without rambling and making a complete fool of myself, I stayed silent and dropped my gaze, not at all surprised when he sidestepped me and blended into the throngs of people making their way toward the gates.

I shook my head, muttering a few choice words under my breath as I started back that way as well, realizing I had to come to terms with the fact today was simply not my day.

"Welcome passengers on Flight 534, we apologize for the delays today, but the cabin crew has just informed me that we look to be ready to start boarding." Finally. The voice of the employee at our gate coming onto the overhead speakers promptly perked everyone in the immediate area up. "We'll start off with anyone boarding in Zone 1, as well as those who require extra assistance or families with young children. Once again, that's only passengers in Zone 1, those who require extra assistance, and families traveling with young children. We'll call the rest of you up shortly, so please sit tight and await further instructions."

But given that nearly everyone was past the point of being fed up, all simply ready to board and get in the air, nobody listened. I, however, stayed where I was—sitting atop my suitcase while leaning against the wall across from the gate. Watching as people began to crowd the check-in desk—pushing and shoving—creating complete and utter madness for the employees attempting to keep things as orderly as possible.

Eventually, when the final boarding call was made and only a few people were left mulling around the check-in desk, I got up and joined the short line. Passport and ticket ready, I handed them off to be scanned before making my way down the rickety bridge leading to the plane.

It was a smaller plane, with only two seats on either side of the aisle, and as I passed all those already seated, I couldn't help but notice half of them anxiously wiggling around in their seats, impatient and waiting for the doors to close. When I reached the middle of the plane, I glanced down at my ticket, double checking my seat number.

27D.

When I spotted the number twenty-seven underneath a half-full overhead compartment, I rolled my luggage to stop, drawing the attention of the man sitting in the aisle seat.

A man that tugged on some thread of familiarity in my mind despite hiding his face underneath a Boston Knights ball cap as he held his phone to his ear.

"Yeah, mom, we're finally boarded and hopefully about to take off, so I've got to hang up." He paused. "I love you, too. I'll call you when we land if it's not too late."

The voice, the build—I couldn't believe my luck could be that bad as to have my seatmate for the flight home be the guy I'd stumbled into hours before—but when he hung up the call and lifted his gaze, I knew it was him.

My teeth found my bottom lip as recognition flared in his eyes. A half smile kicked up on one side of his face as he stood, slipping his phone into the pocket of his trackpants. "I'm guessing you've got the window?" he asked, lifting an eyebrow. I nodded. "You need help with that?" he continued, pointing down to my suitcase when I neglected to give a verbal response.

"No." I cleared my throat, feeling a blush coat my cheeks as I nodded. "I've got it, thanks though."

"No problem."

Taking a step back as I lifted the suitcase into the overhead compartment, he waited until I jammed my bag inside before motioning a bit overdramatically towards the seats.

"After you."

Offering him a small smile, I sidestepped in and took my seat, trying to ignore the way our shoulders and thighs brushed as we dealt with our individual seatbelts and got settled. Or the way a warmth seemed to radiate off him despite the chilled air that circled the cabin. Instead, I attached my gaze to the window, scanning the lights of the tarmac, now much more visible given that the sky had darkened considerably since arriving earlier this afternoon. In the distance, I could see the runway as another plane geared up for takeoff, and felt marginally better knowing the metal tube we were currently inhabiting would be following momentarily.

"So, are you leaving or heading home?"

My eyes flitted towards my seatmate, wondering who he was talking to, only to widen when I realized his head was turned towards me. "Oh," I started, not at all accustomed to starting up conversations with strangers while traveling alone, "I'm, uh, headed home. I just flew out to visit my parents for the holidays." When he nodded in response, leaving me an avenue to bring the conversation to a halt if I wanted, I followed up. "And I'm guessing you're the same? You know, because of the phone call with your mom."

"Yeah," he replied, a lick of amusement at the fact I'd listened in on his conversation. "A short trip, but worth it to see her and the rest of my family." He quirked a brow. "What about you? Ready to get out of California?"

"You mean if we ever actually get in the air?" I mused, all too aware they had yet to shut the door of the plane despite every seat being occupied. "But yeah, is it lame that I'm missing Boston?" I asked. "Like, I miss the daily spectacle of going into work and hanging out with my friends, though I've got to admit, I don't miss the weather."

A deep chuckle escaped his lips. "Not lame, because I feel the same. You get used to going about your day-to-day life, and then when you take a break from routine, no matter how short, everything suddenly feels off balance."

"Exactly."

As I met his understanding eyes, there was a familiarity in his features that I couldn't quite place. And it wasn't just from the moment in the airport, it was something more. Like I'd met him or had seen his face somewhere before. He seemed to be around my age, likely a few years older, but with a quick rake through my mind, I couldn't put my finger on it.

"Though I've got to say," he carried on, "I'd rather the Boston weather right now. Since moving to the north east, celebrating the holidays when the temperature is above freezing and there's no snow on the ground just seems wrong."

"Well then, we can just agree to disagree on that front."

"Fair enough," he said, relaxing back into his seat. "So, why the desire to fly out on New Year's Eve of all days?"

I raised an eyebrow. "Says the guy who's also flying home on New Year's Eve."

"In my defense, I booked this flight because it was meant to land in Boston early enough so I could attend a friend's party, though it looks like that won't be happening." He glanced down at the watch on his wrist. "Plus, I'm meant to be working tomorrow."

"On a stat?"

"Not everyone's lucky enough to work a job that gives you holidays off." He shrugged. "It was hard enough to scrape together the last three days in a row, and that was only because I had business out here anyways."

I was about to ask what it was he did when something clicked into place for me. Where I recognized my seat mate from. I'd seen him countless times over the past three years, skating on television whenever I tuned into a Boston Knights game. Which meant the hat he was wearing wasn't just a piece of memorabilia he was wearing as a fan. No. He was showing off the pride he had for the team he played for.

I was sitting next to Derrick Wellsley, a winger for Boston's professional hockey team. I was keeping up a conversation with Derrick Wellsley. I was flirting with Derrick Wellsley.

What a wild turn of events.

Schooling my emotions, I hoped the way the dots connected in my mind didn't show outwardly, though before I could verbalize anything, I was cut off by a voice echoing throughout the cabin.

"Attention passengers on board Flight 534—" I perked up slightly, peering over the seat in front of me to see the flight attendant at the front of the plane hold the intercom to her lips as she spoke. "—I want to formally apologize to all of you. The pilots have just received word that the all clear to fly they were previously given has been rescinded. This flight has officially been canceled."

I saw the flight attendant visibly wince as nearly every passenger on the plane burst out in a fury of anger—swearing up, right, and center—wondering why the hell we'd boarded in the first place. Which, truthfully, I couldn't help but think as well.

Around me, children cried, parents protested, and the rest of the flight attendants tried to present a united front as they gave instructions for deplaning, but I barely heard a word.

Nothing except from the man who sat beside me.

"Well… it looks like we'll be spending another night on the west coast."

Chapter 2

"**D**ude, I can't believe you're stuck in San Francisco," my roommate, Nyberg, said over the phone as I stepped into the small airport hotel room I'd been given for the night and dropped my carry-on bag. "You're going to miss an epic midnight barbecue at Coach's house."

"I know," I said with a dejected sigh. "But it's not really my choice, man. I didn't ask to have my flight canceled." After tossing my baseball cap onto a side table, I took a couple steps forward to open the curtains. While there'd definitely been better views over the years of away games and tournaments, the fifth floor of the Hyatt was far from the worst. The night a darkened backdrop to the lights and bustling city below. "But Coach was the first one I called back in the airport. I told him I managed to get a seat on the second flight out tomorrow morning, so hopefully I'll be able to make it for pre-game warmups."

Luckily, our game against Washington wasn't until eight 'o'clock tomorrow night, so barring any major delays, I'd be there with time to spare.

"Let's hope that's the case," he said, pausing as I heard him fumble around for something. "Are you at least back at your parents' place for the night?"

I shook my head despite knowing he couldn't see it. "Nope," I replied, sitting down on the edge of the bed. "It wouldn't have made sense to trek all the way back to Santa Clara only to come back super early tomorrow. Plus, I don't want to put a damper on everyone else's New Year's Eve."

"So you're ringing in the new year by yourself?" Nyberg asked, clearly astonished at the turn my night had taken.

"Yeah."

A low whistle traveled down the phone line. "That sucks, man, but hopefully you can find some way to entertain yourself."

Looking around the small box of a room I was currently in—consisting of nothing more than a queen-size bed, a desk, and a fairly ancient looking television set—I knew the way to do that was certainly not here.

"I'll probably head down to the bar in a bit," I said. "Grab a beer or something, maybe see if they've got any games playing."

"Or you can see if there are any women around who catch your eye," he drawled with amusement. "You've got the night off now. Have some fun."

As I held back an eye roll at his suggestion, flashes of red braids, a captivating smile, and beautiful moss green eyes invaded my mind. I'd lost track of my incredibly attractive and hopefully single seat mate back in the craziness of the airport, but as the memory of her came racing back, I couldn't help but wonder if she'd also been put up in this hotel. And if she had, maybe trying to find her and seeing how things would've played out had our conversation on the plane not been cut short wasn't such a bad idea.

"We'll see about that," I said. "And anyways, don't you have somewhere to be?"

"Yeah, yeah, Wellsley, I'm heading out now. I'll be sure to recount your sob story to the guys and tell them you say hi."

I chuckled. "I'll see you tomorrow."

"Later, bud."

Tossing my phone down on the bed, all I could hope for was my luck to do a one-eighty. Otherwise, this night—like most of the day—would end up being a total write off.

Twenty minutes later, the elevator door dinged, sliding open to reveal a nearly empty lobby. There were two workers stationed behind the check-in desk who acknowledged me with a smile as I crossed the room, headed for the small bar I knew to be slightly down the hall and to the left. And as I turned the corner, I knew my choice to shower and switch out my sweats for a clean t-shirt and jeans was the right one, because sitting at the bar, her back toward me, was the woman I'd been hoping to find.

Her naturally red hair had been shaken out of its braids, now cascading down her back, and a pair of wire frames that hadn't been there earlier perched on her nose. She seemed more chilled and at ease as she nursed a beer, not at all bothered by the few other guests scattered around the bar.

Knowing she had yet to notice me, I took the lead, walking the few steps it took to reach the stool next to hers and said, "we've got to stop bumping into each other like this."

Turning to face me, the surprise was evident in her features—arched brows, wide eyes, and slightly parted lips—but it melted away quickly when recognition took its place. "Hey."

"Hey," I echoed, the corners of my lips ticking upward when I nodded down to the free seat. "You mind if I...?"

She shook her head and gestured to the stool. "Go ahead."

Silently thanking someone upstairs that she didn't turn me away, I slid into the spot beside her, though I was immediately pounced on by the bartender before I could get another word out. And out of the corner of my eye, I saw her smirk when I asked him what kind of beer they had, only to get a minute-long spiel about the different kinds of ales and lagers the hotel sourced from local distributors.

"Remind me to just order a Heineken next time," I muttered once the bartender finally left, though I couldn't deny the stout he'd poured looked damn good.

"Don't worry, I made the same mistake when I sat down," she admitted, bringing her glass closer to mine to cheers. The echoing clink of the glasses filled the air around us as I took a long gulp. "So, I guess I'm not the only one who decided taking the airline up on a free hotel room beat heading back home for the night?"

"Guess not," I drawled. "Though that reminds me, I never did get an answer as to why you'd planned to fly back to Boston on New Year's Eve." I lifted a brow. "No boyfriend to cozy up to and kiss at midnight?"

Her lips twitched as she brought her beer up to try and hide her smile. "Smooth."

I shrugged unapologetically. She knew the question was really a way for her to let me know whether or not to back off, and I had no problem admitting that. "I never claimed to be subtle, sweetheart."

"True, I guess professional athletes don't really have subtlety baked into their bones, eh?" My movements froze at the phrase professional athlete, my hand clutching my glass in mid-air. As I slowly met her gaze, I noticed the knowing glint in her eyes. "Thought you could hide that little fact from me?"

"I wasn't necessarily trying to hide it," I admitted, "but it's not normally something I lead with."

"Really?" she asked, a bit of disbelief twisting her words.

"Really. And besides, I'm not that big of a player that most people would recognize me anyways, unless they're from Boston." I took another swig of my beer. "I am curious when you put it together though."

"On the plane, right before the flight got canceled and everything went to shit," she said, and I snorted a laugh. She then gestured to the television behind the bar she'd been watching before I'd interrupted. "Plus, things were pretty much confirmed about twenty minutes ago when one of your goals from earlier in the season was shown on a replay segment."

"The beauty from our game in Toronto last month?"

"That'd be the one."

"Yeah, that was a good night," I said, reminiscing back to the moment one of the Toronto defensemen had tripped me from behind when I'd been on a breakaway. Yet against all odds, I'd still gotten enough power on the shot before I'd faceplanted that the puck sailed cleanly through the goalie's five-hole, becoming the game winner for the night. "But now that you know my name, I feel like we're on a bit of an uneven playing field here since I don't know yours."

She eyed me for a moment, not immediately answering, but from the twinkle in her eyes I could tell she was only trying to make me sweat.

"It's Lia," she finally said.

"Lia," I repeated, the name rolling off my tongue. "Well, Lia, I take it you're a hockey fan?"

"I am... sometimes," she admitted, running her finger along the rim of her glass. "If I'm being honest, I'm actually more of a football fan." The cockiness I knew to be present in my grin immediately vanished, causing Lia to throw her head back with laughter. "What? Didn't expect that?"

I shook my head slowly with an ounce of disbelief and said, "Honestly, no. These days it's rare to find a woman who's interested in hockey, let alone other sports."

"Then clearly you're looking in the wrong places."

"Clearly."

She quirked a brow. "Though I find it hard to believe it's hard to find women interested in hockey. Isn't the term puck bunny still a thing?"

"You're right," I conceded with a snort of a laugh. "I stand correct-ed, but those women are usually interested in one thing, and it's not what I can do out on the ice."

"Noted."

With the moment of silence, I wondered if I'd taken things one step too far, but for the second time tonight, Lia surprised me. Instead of being put off or judgemental, she looked downright amused as she took a sip of her beer to hide the wry tilt of her lips.

"I'm curious though," I started, "what drew you to football over anything else?"

"My dad," she said simply, her smile softening. "I remember my mom telling me that when I was little I would sit with my dad on the couch on Sundays when San Francisco was playing and essentially be his copycat. When he'd cheer, so would I, and when he'd yell at the TV, I would too. I obviously never knew what was going on until I got older and he explained all the rules to me, but it became a tradition for the two of us to watch games on Sundays while my mom would run errands. There's actually a picture framed in my parent's living room from the last Sunday game we watched together before I moved out east—matching jerseys and all."

"Cute," I mused, causing her to lean over and nudge her shoulder with mine. "I'm guessing you're a ride or die fan then?"

"For football, yes, but don't worry, I only started watching hockey a few years back when two of my friends in Boston kept convincing me to go to games with them, so I cheer for the Knights."

Mocking a sigh of relief, I turned my chair slightly to fully face her, my knees less than an inch away from touching her thigh. "Thank fuck for that. Imagine if you were a Washington Eagles fan, or worse—" I shuttered. "—a Florida Sharks fan."

"Funnily enough, that was actually the last game I went to see live, when you played them back in October."

I grimaced as I lifted my glass to take a long gulp, the awful memory of that night coming back to me. "You mean the night when our team just couldn't get things together?"

"If that's what you call your teammates getting a boat load of penalties and then ending the game down seven, then yes, that night."

"Oof, way to rub salt on the wound, Lia."

An airy laugh escaped her lips. "Sorry, though you should know better than most that some nights just suck, whether it's due to things not syncing up or plain bad luck. But all those nights prove is that the choice comes down on you to decide how to turn things around after the fact."

Logically, I knew she was talking about hockey—about how teams had to learn from their mistakes and grow—but I couldn't help but take a second meaning from her words. Maybe I was reading too far into things, but I also got the sense that she was referencing the situation we were in right now. How the timing of the storm sweeping across the middle of the country sucked and there was nothing we could do about the hand we'd been dealt, but we could choose to focus on the sliver of positives if we wanted.

Like how the two of us had been brought together, if only for a night.

And the more we chatted, the more down to Earth and easy-going I found her. There was something about her—some underlying quality I couldn't quite put my finger on—that made talking about anything seem natural and not at all awkward despite not really knowing each other.

Then on top of that, the longer we sat there, the more the sexual tension between us grew. I could feel it in the glances we exchanged every couple of minutes, in the way our arms and legs brushed when one of us deliberately shifted in our chairs, and as we both gradually began leaning closer, as if the rest of the bar was empty and we had the entire space to ourselves.

Until we were interrupted, that is.

"Champagne?" the bartender asked, holding a bottle of bubbly up as he looked between us. "Everyone gets one glass on the house tonight."

"Yes please," Lia answered quickly, biting her bottom lip gently as if she'd been caught doing something she wasn't meant to be.

And as I opened my mouth to respond, the words never came, because my gaze caught the television behind the bar. What had once been broadcasting sports highlights was now a countdown to midnight—saying there was less than half an hour to go—making me realize just how long the two of us had been sitting here.

"And you?" the bartender asked, waiting with an eyebrow raised.

"Oh, sorry," I said, pulling my focus away from the screen. "Yeah, I'll have some, thanks."

After pouring enough to fill two champagne flutes halfway, he replaced our empty glasses with the bubbly and wished us a happy new year before making the rounds to the rest of the guests.

"I didn't realize it'd gotten so late," Lia said, her eyes meeting mine with a heat that was dimmed slightly by an accompanying shyness.

"Neither did I," I replied, not letting my gaze drop, but pausing as I figured out the best way to lead our night into a new direction. After taking a small sip of champagne, I reached my free hand out and rested it across the back of her chair. "And I don't know about you, but I think this champagne would taste better away from prying eyes." I let the underlying invitation hang between us for a few seconds, trying to gauge her reaction, and when I saw the smallest uptick of her lips, the fire of attraction in my chest grew. "So, what do you say?"

"Lead the way."

Chapter 3

U nnerving, but in a good way.

That was the only way to describe the feeling coursing through my veins as I stepped into the hotel elevator with Derrick, champagne in hand, while his free hand warmed the base of my spine.

As the doors began to close, I pulled my bottom lip in between my teeth, all too aware we were about to be alone for the first time. Completely and utterly alone. A vision of him slowly backing me up against the wall invaded my mind. Of our drinks falling to the ground as his hands came to rest on either side of my head. Of him bending down to capture my lips with his own. Of our tongues dancing, our hands exploring, and our bodies moving against one another in an accelerated rhythm until the doors opened once more.

But the fantasy, or, uh, vision, was quickly derailed as a hand shot out to stop the elevator door from closing.

Derrick's hand fell from my back—though the warmth from his touch lingered—as a woman in her mid-to-late sixties stepped in with us, hitting the button for the ninth floor before looking our way. "Now what are you two young things doing at an airport hotel on New Year's Eve?"

Unable to come up with an answer other than 'we're about to have sex!', I glanced at Derrick to see the corner of his mouth twitch upward, as if he knew exactly what I was thinking.

"Our flight back to Boston was canceled because of a storm en route," he replied as the elevator began to rise. "How about you?"

"Oh, my hubby and I are headed out early to Seattle tomorrow morning to visit our grandchildren since they were away over Christmas, so we thought we'd camp out here tonight instead of waking up so damn early."

There was a moment of silence as I nodded in understanding, the fingers of my left hand tapping nervously against my thigh as we came to a stop at the fifth floor.

"Happy new year," I finally managed to say before stepping out. Turning back to smile at her, I continued. "And hopefully everything goes alright with your flight tomorrow."

"You as well," she replied cheerily. "And remember, there's a whole lot of fun that can be had in a hotel room."

Her words were punctuated with a wink as the door slid shut, causing a red tint to color my cheeks. "Were we that obvious?" I asked, gobsmacked.

There was no reply, only his deep chuckle as Derrick led me down the hall. In a handful of steps, we reached his room and with a quick flash of his key card, the door unlocked, and he gestured me inside.

And that was when my confidence began to dim.

There was nothing special about the room, in fact, it was the exact same as my own a floor below. Except mine didn't have Derrick's luggage tossed in the corner beside the bed. Nor did I remember it having this nice of a view. With the curtains pulled to the side, the lights of the city were vibrant against the darkened sky and the moon—now high in the sky—cast a subtle, silver glow into the room. It was sensual. Enticing. Another reminder about what was about to happen.

"I can close those if you want."

Without even realizing, I'd moved further into the room, facing away from Derrick as I stood at the foot of the bed. "No," I said, cringing at the slight crack to my voice despite the whispered tone. "This is fine."

"You sure?" he asked, and I didn't respond. My pulse pounded as I heard him shuffle closer; until he was right behind me. Separated by no more than a few inches, I felt the warmth of his chest radiating against my back as his free hand reached out to gently caress my hip. "Lia, are you one hundred percent cool with this?" His voice was a low rumble against my ear. "Because if you're not, we can just head back down to the bar."

Strangely enough, those words caused the second thoughts roaming my mind to vanish. His reassurance that this didn't need to happen if I was no longer into it was the exact reason I wanted it to. There was no denying he was a decent guy on top of being any woman's fantasy, and with his attention solely on me for the night, I intended to take make the most of it.

After all, I was single and totally down to mingle.

Giving into temptation, I turned to face him, allowing my eyes to drop to his lips as I lifted my glass. "I'm sure."

I saw the flash of heat in his eyes as he tapped his glass against mine, the echoing clink prompting the hair on my arms to rise. One long gulp was all it took for the last drops of champagne to disappear before everything changed. What had been a slow moving seduction brewing since the first moment we'd bumped into each other in the airport changed to a scorching need as our lips came together frantically.

My arms wrapped around his waist as his fingers tangled in my hair, pulling me closer as his tongue swept across my bottom lip. With a moan on my account, the kiss deepened, adding fuel to the flames of desire in my chest. And just when I thought I couldn't take it any longer, Derrick tore his mouth from mine and began peppering kisses down my neck. Delving lower with each sweep—the sensitive skin underneath my ear, my collarbone, my shoulder, the neckline of my long sleeve t-shirt that definitely wasn't sexy but was making me feel so as the material stretched downwards.

With nearly every nerve in my body on high alert, and my pants filling the air around us, I grabbed his face, kissing him fiercely, in need of something... more.

Pulling back and breathing heavy, my hands coasted slowly over his broad shoulders and the material covering them. Tight enough to show off the muscles he'd clearly worked hard for, there was still enough slack that the shirt bunched in my grasp as I reached his biceps and flicked my eyes up to meet his.

"I think it's time for this to come off. Now."

There was no objection as the corner of his mouth curved upward in a sultry smirk. "You've got it." But he didn't comply right away, instead, reaching up to tap the side of my glasses I'd forgotten I was even wearing, so used to having contacts in. "As long as these come off too."

Not having any need for them for the rest of the night, I took my glasses off and placed them safely to the side before quirking a brow, silently telling him it was his turn.

In one swift movement, his shirt was thrown carelessly to the side and his arms circled my waist, once again closing the space between us. In a frenzy of lips and tongue, I couldn't help but revel in the trail of heat that rose on my skin when his touch drifted lower, skimming the sliver of bare skin at my waist before coasting over my ass and stopping on my thighs.

Bending down to my height and squeezing, I was more than happy to oblige with his prompting as he yanked both of my legs around his waist and moved us two steps sideways until we fell softly onto the bed.

With me on top.

Slowing my kisses to a teasing pace, I leaned back so that my thighs nestled around his hips. Taking the chance to admire his exposed chest, my fingers appeared dainty as they slowly moved over every ridge, pausing to inspect a small scripted tattoo of the right side of his abdomen.

Never give up. Always keep pushing.

"Any significance behind this?"

"Just something my dad used to say when I was a kid trying to find my footing on the ice." There was a lightness in his eyes as I glanced up at his face. "Plus, it covers a scar I got during high school when I got a skate to this stomach."

A breezy laugh escaped him as I cringed, though when I scooted down his body to get a closer look, the room became quiet once more. Like he was holding his breath. Waiting until I found the tiny, uneven line underneath the inked words and brought my lips to it.

Growling in satisfaction, Derrick's hips rose off the bed, making me grin as I continued to explore his abs with my mouth. Tracing them with my tongue, I was only encouraged by the sounds filling the room, and boldly grazed my hand over the impressive bulge in his jeans before popping open the button and unzipping him.

"Lia..."

"Shh," I said, flicking my eyes to meet his as I tried my best to push the fabric of his pants down his legs. "Don't worry, I want to."

There were no more objections, though there was a bit of fumbling as the two of us quickly worked together to rid him of his jeans and boxers before he laid back down, his cock fully erect.

My hand was barely big enough to wrap around him entirely, but I made it work, working him over with a few experimental pumps before prompting a hiss of pleasure when my lips closed around the tip.

"Is this good?" I asked after licking the length of his shaft and massaging the base.

"Yes, fuck." His hips pumped upward as my tongue flattened against the head. "Anything you do with your mouth is fucking fantastic."

"Good to know."

Empowered, I moaned around him and began to take him deeper, getting into a rhythm that he seemed to enjoy if the groans filling the room were anything to go by. Though when his hand lifted from the sheets and tangled in my hair, instead of encouraging me like I expected, he pulled lightly to get my attention.

"As much as I'm loving what you're doing—" In one swift movement that I could not for the life of me follow, I suddenly found myself lying on my back with Derrick hovering me. Naked. "—we're a little unmatched when it comes to clothes."

"Well, you see," I started, suddenly getting nervous again, knowing what I had on underneath these clothes, "I didn't plan on sleeping with you tonight."

He lifted an eyebrow, his hand hovering above the waistline of my jeans. "No?" he asked. "You sure you didn't go down to the bar looking for me?"

I gulped, because I hadn't thought much about it. I figured I'd finally had enough of this day and—after calling my parents and telling them not to worry about me—had just needed a drink. To simply chill out as the year came to an end. But maybe, just maybe, I could remember feeling a tug in my gut that told me to change into something a little more presentable. To dab on a bit of lip gloss and a few swipes of mascara before heading down to the lobby.

"Because let me tell you something Lia," he continued, his tone husky and low. "I went down there hoping to find you."

The words short-circuited every logical train of thought as the button to my jeans snapped open and his hand slowly slid the material down my legs. Revealing the pair of underwear I'd designated for what was supposed to be a travel day—baby blue boy shorts with cartoon giraffes.

Derrick's eyes lit up with silent laughter. "Cute."

I narrowed my eyes playfully, though when I opened my mouth to tell him not to say one more word, he silenced me with his lips. I could feel his calloused fingers pulling at my boy shorts, shifting them down my legs as his tongue explored my mouth. An unperfect kiss that was urgent and hungry, reigniting the wanting within me.

When his hands wrapped around my now-bare thighs, stopping the desperate rocking motion of my hips, I knew something more was coming. And when he tore his mouth from mine, only to bring it to the sensitive skin of my inner thigh—rewarding me with a torturous combination of kisses and licks—I succumbed to the intoxicating sensations.

With one finger, then two, he tried his best to read my body's responses, not at all perturbed by my hands in his hair, guiding him to where I needed him. A yelp of ecstasy escaped me when he finally brought his mouth down on me, focusing his attention on the small bundle of nerves. His tongue moved in slow, concise circles, causing my legs to shake and the pleasure between my thighs to build, bringing me closer to the edge. Knowing there was no way I was holding on much longer, I moved my hips in the exact way I needed to get my release, and moments later, when his lips closed around my swollen bud and he sucked hard, I fell apart.

There was no silencing the sounds that left my lips and echoed off the walls around us, but I didn't care, reveling in the bliss that coursed through my body.

Things slowed down as he inched back up my body, stopping along the way to rid my upper body of clothes and drop open mouthed kisses along my skin. On my hip, my stomach, each breast, my collarbone, and finally my lips.

Breathing heavily, I pulled back. "Please tell me you have a condom."

Nodding, Derrick reached down to where his pants had been thrown and grabbed his wallet from one of the pockets, pulling out two packets of foil.

I raised an eyebrow, amused. "Two, eh?"

Grinning, he shrugged. "You never know when you'll need them."

Tossing one to the side, he tore the other open and quickly sheathed himself before crawling back over me. With one hand, he pushed the stray hairs away from my face, cupping my cheek. "You know," he started, moving his hips to line us up perfectly, circling the tip of his cock around my opening, "I'm not that mad our flight was canceled anymore."

He inched forward slowly and I shuddered, in tune to every small movement he made before reaching the hilt. Dropping his forehead to my shoulder, a groan sounded from the back of his throat, causing my grip on his biceps to tighten.

"You know," I said, repeating his words as my hips involuntarily moved to find the best friction, "this would be a whole lot better if you moved."

His chest shook as he chuckled, pushing up on his forearms so I could see his wicked smile. "Well, honey, you asked for it."

With the first thrust—which consisted of him pulling nearly all the way out before slamming home again—I was no longer complaining. Instead, I was making sounds I couldn't even comprehend as Derrick moved at a pace that was pure perfection, yet painstakingly slow at the same time to draw out the pressure building between my legs.

His strong, warm hands glided across my skin confidently, as if there was an underlying instinct telling him which parts of my body he needed to focus on. Particularly the spot above my right hip where he circled his thumb consistently as his lips nipped at a spot underneath my left ear.

And when that was no longer enough, I wrapped my legs around his hips, creating a new angle where his thrusts began hitting the spot I needed them to. Over and over again. Soon enough, I felt the wave of another orgasm building and couldn't stop the encouraging mumbles that left my lips, telling Derrick not to stop as he continued to pound into me; harder and with more power than before. As if he too was on the edge and desperate for release.

Crying out, I clutched the sheets and arched my back, barely able to register when Derrick hit his climax too, because I was so overwhelmed with the hormones pulsing through every inch of my body.

There was no question about it, I was one hundred percent satisfied.

Opening my eyes as Derrick's weight shifted on top of me, I noticed the equally satiated expression his featured held.

"That was..." I said, trailing off in a pant, not able to compute the right word for what had just happened.

Though I knew it was somewhere between magnificent, gratifying, and mind-blowing.

Just as out of breath as I was, Derrick nodded in agreement. "Yeah, it was."

After dropping a quick kiss to my lips, he rolled off me and stood, padding across the room to dispose of the condom in the bathroom, and leaving me to marvel at the astonishing turn of events this day had taken. If there hadn't have been a storm that canceled our flight, we would've been seat mates, nothing more, and I would've missed out on this seriously killer sex that had more than made up for my five-month dry spell.

Was it wrong to be thankful the weather had decided to crap out on us? Because if it was, I didn't want to be right.

Next to me, the bed dipped when Derrick returned, and his fingers gently skimmed my own beneath the sheets I'd wiggled under. "Happy new year, Lia."

Turning my gaze to the small digital clock on the nightstand, sure enough, I could make out the blurry numbers to see it was five minutes past midnight. Which meant the year had started off with a bang, literally.

Definitely not the worst way to bring in the new year.

Rolling back to face him, I splayed my fingers against his chest, hoping it wasn't just me who was ready for another round. "Happy new year to you, too."

The burst of lust in his eyes told me I definitely wasn't alone, and when his hands came up to cup my breasts before his mouth closed around a puckered nipple, I knew I was in for a long night.

Chapter 4

"Derrick Wellsley?" Esme asked, making sure she'd heard right. "As in the man who plays for the Boston Knights? The tall, dark, and handsome winger that even I'd do if I was remotely interested in men?"

Unable to keep the heat from rising to my cheeks, I took a sip of my iced coffee as I nodded, also casting my eyes around the café to make sure nobody was eavesdropping.

It'd been three days since I'd woken up naked in Derrick's hotel room, early enough that the sun was barely high enough to chase away the darkness. But one ray had met my tired eyes as I rolled over to see the man beside me still dead asleep, his arms tucked underneath his pillow and only a sheet covering the lower half of his body. Knowing it was time to make my exit, I'd looked my fill one last time—how could I not—before slipping out of bed. I'd tiptoed around the room, careful not to wake him as I collected my clothes, threw them on, and used the pen and notepad the hotel provided to scribble a quick note to him before sneaking out.

Maybe it wasn't the most tactful, but I hadn't wanted to draw it out and make things awkward. A clean break had seemed best, especially after I realized that we were, in fact, not on the same flight home.

It was a great night, but that was all it was. One night. There was no use trying to make it into something more.

"Damn." Esme's eyes were wide as she shook her head in amazement. "I can't believe it."

"Honestly, I can't either," I admitted.

I'd had plenty of flashbacks over the last couple of days, almost all of them from the moments before one of the four orgasms Derrick had gifted me. It was honestly a lot for my brain to handle, not being one who frequented all-night sex marathons. Not with my past boyfriends, who were typically once-a-night type guys unless it was a special occasion, and certainly not with strangers. I'd only had one other one-night-stand in my life, during a girls' trip to the Caribbean a few years back, and it certainly hadn't been anything to write home about. But this—Derrick—had been fantastic in bed, and it was a bit of a bummer to realize I wouldn't be getting a repeat. Which was why my best friends were only now learning about it at our weekly Monday morning coffee date. It took time to process.

"And you're sure there's no chance for a repeat?"

I shook my head. "Considering we didn't exchange numbers and I snuck out while he was sleeping, I'm going to go with no."

"Well you're both in Boston, so never say never," Esme quipped. "This city is smaller than people think, so there's always a chance of running into him."

"But it's a pretty small chance," Harper added. She was the third member of our trio, and also happened to be Esme's girlfriend. With her arm slung over the back of Esme's chair, she'd remained silent as I recounted the majority of my sexcapade, but her facial features had certainly shown her surprise and amusement. "If I were in your shoes, I would be more worried about reconnecting with Miles."

I rolled my eyes. "And why is that?" I asked, though I already knew the answer.

Since starting my PhD five years ago, Miles and I have shared an office on the Harvard campus, as well as lab space under the same supervising professor. As part of the research team working on the creation of fully-functioning artificial cells, our work frequently put us in close quarters, and while we have slightly different areas of expertise and study, there are times we need the other to share results of our individual experiments to help the other along in their research.

And despite being nothing but friends since we'd met, Harper and Esme couldn't help but point out his 'obvious' crush on me. I, however, knew there was nothing between us. Sure, he'd asked me out after knowing me for a month all those years ago, but after quickly shutting him down—nicely, of course—there hadn't been any hint of him wanting to be anything more. He'd had girlfriends over the years and I'd had boyfriends. We worked together, and a couple times a month we got drinks or takeout when we both stuck around the lab late, but that was it.

Yet my friends didn't want to believe it. That, or they simply liked having something to tease me about.

Harper's irises gleamed with mirth. "Because this is it. You're both set to give your final defense before the end of the term and then you won't be seeing each other unless you purposefully make plans. He won't be able to stay late in the lab to chat with you or schedule experiments on the same day anymore. After all, you're both single, so if he's going to make a move—which I bet he will—it'll be soon."

"Now you're just being dramatic. There's no way that'll happen."

"Especially because she's hung up on a certain hockey stud," Esme cut in, wiggling her eyebrows suggestively. "Who, according to Lia here, is pretty hung himself."

Harper snorted out a laugh as I tried to shush her. "Announce that to the world why don't you?" I mumbled before finishing off my drink. "And I'm not hung up on anyone. It was just sex."

"Really good sex, apparently."

"Yeah, but like I said, it was a one-time thing. Even if I had gotten his number, I don't think I'd use it. At least not any time soon." My hands rested atop the table, my drink now pushed to the side as I fidgeted and tapped my nails on the wood. "These next couple months are going to be crucial if I'm going to be ready for my defense, and I can't have anything jeopardizing that."

"We get that, Lia, don't worry," Harper said, reaching across the table to place a hand on mine.

"Yeah," Esme agreed, her mouth curving into a soft smile. "We'll be there in April to watch you kick ass at your defense, but we also don't want you locking yourself in your lab like you did back in first year. Your team knows you work hard, so there's no reason you shouldn't be able to let loose once in a while."

Starting my PhD at twenty-one had been a big deal—both to me and my family. As the adopted daughter of the owners of San Francisco's most authentic Mexican restaurant, I'd been the first of the family to graduate high school, let alone college. Getting accepted into Harvard's esteemed graduate program right out of undergrad had been the chance of a lifetime, and I hadn't wanted to lose my scholarships or end up a disappointment.

Unfortunately, that kind of pressure had prompted me to go overboard—to volunteer for as much lab work as possible, to over enroll in classes, and to spend any free moment with my head in a textbook. The obsession to achieve that quickly began causing problems. Problems I hadn't realized were actually damaging my work until I met Esme, who'd helped me come to my senses and had stuck by my side ever since.

"Trust me, I won't be returning to the dark times any time soon," I said with reassurance. "Besides, with you guys at my back, there's always fun to be had."

"Damn straight."

Chuckling, I checked the time on my phone only to see it was approaching eight thirty, and I had a meeting with my supervising professor at nine. "Speaking of my defense, I should get going. Don't want to be late on my first day back."

"Yeah, we've got to get going too," Harper said. "Did you need a ride, or did you drive today?"

I shook my head as I stood, buttoning up my coat. It was below freezing this morning, so there was no way I was walking if I could help it. "Luckily, my car decided to start, so I'm good."

"You really do need to get a new car," Harper mused.

It wasn't that my 2004 Toyota Corolla was bad, it was just... temperamental. "Maybe in a few months when I know that I have a full-time job."

"You will, don't worry," Esme said encouragingly as we exited the café and were blasted with the chilled winter air. "We're parked around the block, but let us know how your first day back goes, yeah?"

"Will do."

"You're teaching the Introduction to Cells and Tissues class to the undergraduates this term, correct? On Tuesdays and Thursdays?"

I nodded as I sat across from Professor Klein in her office, going over my plans for my final term. "Yes. I submitted my course plan to the faculty before Christmas and it was approved, so I'll be ready to go tomorrow."

"Any nerves? Or last-minute things you want to go over?"

"I think I'm good to go, honestly. I mean, it'll definitely be a little nerve-racking knowing the students will be relying on me in such a big capacity, but I'm also excited to get started."

Her head bobbed in approval, she jotted something down on her notepad quickly. "That's good to hear. Especially considering this will be good experience should you still wish to apply for a lecturing spot here after graduation in the spring. Is that still your plan?"

"It is."

"Well then, I wish you the best of luck." The corner of her eyes crinkled with a smile. "But do feel comfortable coming to me if you need guidance when it comes to your students or the examinations."

"I will, thank you."

"Is there anything else we need to go over before you head to the lab?"

I didn't believe there was, as we'd already gone over the schedule for my last class, which I was enrolled in on Friday mornings, and she'd approved my preliminary request for lab time. "I think we're all good, Professor," I said, standing from my seat and collecting my things. "Though I did put in a request at the end of last term for additional equipment and more cell clusters to continue extracting DNA and moving forward with my final round of tests. I was told they were granted, so I'll be doing inventory before starting the write up for my experiment plan."

"Everything should be there," she reaffirmed, "and if you can get a draft on my desk before I leave tonight, we can sit down tomorrow and make sure everything is prepped to go for Wednesday."

"Great."

"Oh, and Lia?" I looked back over my shoulder, having already started to make my exit. "I hope you had a good time with your family over the holidays."

"Thanks, I did, and now I'm ready to get back to work."

And half an hour later, that's exactly what I had done. Donning my lab coat and glasses, I'd tossed my hair into a high ponytail before printing out the list I'd submitted weeks ago, wanting to check everything I needed for the term had been ordered and stocked. And most importantly, that nothing was damaged.

Alone in the lab, I had my headphones in to zero in on the task at hand. I'd already checked the fridges in the back room to confirm all my cells had been stocked and had now moved on to the glassware cupboards. The new microscope slides looked good, as did the few beaker replacements we'd needed, but when I reached up on my tiptoes to pull out the new box of mini test tubes, I felt a tap on my shoulder and jumped.

"Shit," I said, cringing as I heard the clang of glass echo over my music. Pulling my headphones out, I turned to see an apologetic Miles.

"Sorry, Lia," he said, rubbing the back of his neck. "I thought you could hear me coming, or I wouldn't have snuck up on you."

I sighed, hoping the protective sleeves had done their job and none of the tubes had shattered. "It's fine Miles, don't worry." The embarrassed tinge to his olive skin began to fade when I noticed the messenger bag slung over his shoulder. "You coming back from teaching?"

"Yeah, and I think it went well. Though it was only the first day, so we'll see how the rest of the term goes." A small grin blossomed as he raked his fingers through his black hair. "But enough about me. What about you? How's this term looking for you, and how was your vacation?"

"I start teaching tomorrow, and then besides my one class, I'll be in the lab most of the time," I explained. "And my vacation was good." I cracked a smile. "I only looked at my research twice, if that tells you anything."

"I feel that." A laugh rumbled his chest. "But I'll let you get back to it," he said, gesturing to the test tube box on the counter. Though after a few steps, he turned back around. "Actually, I had one more thing I wanted to talk to you about."

When I saw a spark of hopefulness in his eyes, unease began to creep its way into my chest. With Harper's word still floating in my head, saying if he's going to make a move, it'll be soon, all I could do was hope he wasn't about to make the next four months extremely awkward by asking me out.

"What is it?" I asked, making sure to mark my expression.

"I was thinking we could get together some time over the next week or two—" Oh no. "—and link up with our research." I expelled a slow, relieved breath. "With both our defenses coming up, I thought it'd be useful to swap notes. You know, give each other another set of eyes to point out any inconsistencies or come up questions that might help the other along." He lifted an eyebrow. "So, what do you say?"

"Yeah, that sounds good," I replied. "If you check the lab schedule, I'm free most afternoons, so just let me know when you want to sit down and chat."

"Great, I'll text you," he chirped, backing away as he headed for our office on the other side of the lab.

Leaving me to deal with a possibly broken set of test tubes and half-finished inventory checklist. Back to business indeed.

Chapter 5

The loud chirp of a whistle sounded. "Wellsley, you're up."

I barely heard the assistant offensive coach, solely focused on the task at hand as I jumped over the boards and took my second run through the obstacle course laid out on the ice. Starting off with one fast lap around the rink, my blades glided swiftly; a movement as routine as walking to me after all these years.

When I crossed the center red line, I snagged a puck from the pile to the side and began to weave my way through the sequence of pylons scattered on one side of the ice. There were twenty of them, all fairly close together, but my stick handling was second nature and in about ten seconds I was through, then pushing myself hard to the other end of the ice where Nyberg waited, ready between the pipes.

Looking for the perfect shot, I saw that he was ready on nearly every level. His stance was strong, protecting much of the net, and on his feet, he was agile. Waiting for me to make a move, his eyes flicked between the puck and my face. I knew I had a tell—relying on my core muscles and right side as I bent over my stick to shoot—so, after formulating a plan of action, I did exactly what was expected of me.

With a short wind up and quick release, my wrist shot flew off my stick and hit its mark—about two inches above where his blocker had been. It was an easy save, but I wasn't hoping for a goal. I'd been after the rebound, and as the puck bounced back onto the ice, albeit a little farther to the left than I would've liked, I got my chance.

I knocked a one timer towards the top of the net, swore under my breath when Nyberg deftly slid across the crease to block it.

He chuckled through his headgear as I rounded the back of the net, heading back for the bench. "Better luck next time."

Whistle after whistle sounded as the rest of the team gave the course one more go, with only a few hitting the back of the net as Coach alternated goalies. And when the drill ended, leaving me without a goal, I was more determined to kick it into high gear for the half-hour scrimmage that ended our practice.

The division of players was fair, with players from all four lines mixed among teams, and while everyone knew to take it easy on the hits, we all still wanted to give it our all.

It took a few shifts, but I settled into my groove when I found myself rushing down the ice next to Brookes, who I was used to playing with on game nights. The puck bounced back and forth between our sticks as we deked out the defensemen, and this time, when I saw the open five-hole and took a shot, it sailed cleanly across the goal line.

Followed by another bullet to the top corner two shifts later, which secured our team the win at 5-4 as practice came to a close.

"Okay, bring it in men," Coach said from center ice, his voice echoing throughout the arena. Most of us sucking wind after hours of skating, we glided slowly towards him and waited for his parting words. "After Wednesday's win in Dallas, I was proud to see you guys putting the same level of effort into today's practice. If we come out here tomorrow night with this kind of morale, we'll have the fans on our side when we show Montreal that them getting the best of us the last time we met was a fluke." There were whistles and hoots in agreement. "Now get out of here," Coach said, waving towards the tunnel. "And I better see you all here tomorrow, ready and hungry for a win."

"Knights on three!" Simmons, our captain, yelled.

"One, two, three, Knights!"

My adrenaline was still flowing as I followed my teammates off the ice, bumping gloves with the coaching staff as I passed them.

"Hey," one of the assistant coaches said, catching my attention as I skated by. "Great work out there in the scrimmage today."

"Thanks."

Though I knew one compliment or one good practice—hell, even a streak of good games—couldn't keep my spot on the team safe. My agent had told me there'd been rumblings of trading me over the summer, and while nothing had manifested yet, that didn't put me in the clear. Not until the trade deadline passed at the end of February. Because if the front office wanted to switch things up and bring in new meat, there was nothing I could do to change their minds.

Nothing other than play my best and let the chips fall where they may.

These thoughts circled my head as I entered the locker room and stripped out of my equipment, not taking time to stop and shoot the shit with my teammates before grabbing a towel and heading for the showers. Thankfully, the spray was hot enough to shove most of my worries away, and the steam did wonders to rid me of telltale reek of hard work.

"Yo, did you guys see Leonard's hat trick against Florida last night?" Mackay said, his voice carrying into the showers as I dried off, wrapping my towel around my waist.

"It was definitely a beauty."

"Especially that second goal. A rocket right off the inside of the post."

"And maybe it'll be good for us," I cut in, starting to dress. "It's doubtful lightning like that strikes twice in a row."

"Wellsley's right," Simmons said, clapping me on the shoulder. Somehow, even though I'd been the first to hit the showers, he was already dressed and packed to leave. "If the guy's not at top capacity tomorrow and we can get an edge over their starting defensive line, we'll have a great shot at securing another W."

"Damn straight," I said, easily going along with the handshake he offered. "See you tomorrow?"

"Bright and early for game film."

The locker room slowly began to dwindle down once our captain made his exit, though since Nyberg and I carpooled most days—there was no need to take two cars to and from the same place—I was left waiting for him.

"Dude," he said, minutes later when he was finally ready to go. He combed his fingers through his damp hair. "I totally blanked that I'm meant to swing by Harvard to chat with their goalie. Coach set it up last week, since the guy is a senior and hoping to be an unrestricted free agent after graduation, especially with the team set to make the Frozen Four for the second time. So, I can either quickly swing by the apartment and drop you off, or—"

"Don't worry about it, I'll come with you," I said, tossing my gym bag over my shoulder. Though I held out my hand for his keys. "But I'm driving."

"Did Orlov say anything about his quad still acting up?" Nyberg said from the passenger seat as I drove into Harvard Square, wanting to snag a free spot instead of paying the fees on campus and at the arena.

"Yeah." He'd dived in front of a hard shot in our last game, but while the puck had bounced off his pads, the speed of it had brought the pain with it. "The doctors have said it's just a bruise, but if he's still gritting his teeth after icing it tonight, he'll be sitting tomorrow."

"Rough."

"I'm guessing Coach already has Carter on speed dial, since that's who usually gets the call."

"And he's been playing well this season, so I don't think it'll put us back too far."

I agreed. "It'll be fine. Montreal won't know what's hit them."

Spotting the parking garage I'd been looking for, I turned in and saw it wasn't as busy as I expected. Though it had also just gone five, so a lot of people must've already headed home for the night. Making it that much easier to find an open spot on the first level, where I backed in Nyberg's SUV and cut the engine.

"So, not that I don't enjoy the company," Nyberg drawled as we climbed out the car and headed for the street, "but shouldn't you have a date or something lined up for tonight? I mean, didn't that blonde girl at the bar last weekend slip you her number? What happened?"

Charlie, said blonde girl, had indeed given me her number after we'd spent the better part of the night feeling each other up in the back corner of the bar. The problem, however, laid in the chemistry. Or lack thereof. With only two beers in me, I'd tried to get into it—kissing her hard as her hands explored underneath my shirt—but there'd been no will to move things further until another face popped into my head.

Another face, from another bar. Red hair, pink lips, and green eyes that brought me back to a night I desperately wanted to repeat. Sex with Lia had been off the charts and I'd woken up the next morning intending to ask to see her again, only to find myself alone with a note on her pillow.

Thanks for a great night.

Five words that were enough to let me know she wasn't interested in a repeat. Something my brain clearly hadn't registered in the nearly two weeks that had passed since then.

And while I knew I could've easily called Charlie to set up a date, I wasn't that much of an asshole. When I brought women out, or to bed, it was about them as much as me.

"There was nothing there," I said, my explanation short. Shrugging my shoulders, I tucked my hands away from the cold. The wind was rough and damp off the water as we crossed the bridge that led to where the athletic complex, not helped at all by the light snow that began to fall. "It wouldn't have been worth it, so all my plans for tonight consisted of was watching a game with a beer in my hand."

"Sure looked like there was enough there to me, if you know what I mean," he replied suggestively, nudging my arm. Of course he was referencing her rack. I rolled my eyes and he chuckled.

"But don't worry, we'll find you someone this weekend. Especially if we're celebrating two more wins."

"Which we better be, so don't choke in net," I chirped back, laughing as I turned my head to check for cars, only to see a gorgeous redhead bundled up on the other side of the street.

A familiar gorgeous redhead.

Flashbacks of her at the hotel bar grinning and laughing hit me, followed closely by scenes that had replayed several times over the last few weeks while I'd been alone in the shower. Of her straddling me. Of her flushed face after orgasming for the third time. Of her mouth bringing me to the brink of my own release.

"Derrick, you okay, man?"

I shook myself out of it, only to see Nyberg's brows drawn together in confusion a few steps in front of me. "Sorry, I just thought I saw..." I trailed off, glancing back to where I thought I'd seen Lia. But there was nobody there. "Never mind, I'm good."

"You sure?"

I needed to be, because this was getting ridiculous. I'd been rejected before, it wasn't anything new, so I just had to figure out a way to get this woman out of my head. Preferably before it started affecting other things in my life, like my game.

"Yeah, don't worry." I clapped him on the shoulder as we reached the arena. "Now, let's go see if this goalie's got what it takes."

Seeing as the Knights used the Harvard facilities whenever there was a conflict for ice time, we knew our way around. After a quick hello to the coach, who was surprised his player was getting a two-for-one deal with us, he led us to the weight room, which was empty except for the guy we were looking for.

Tall, muscular, and bearded, he certainly looked in good enough to shape to grab the attention of scouts. And on top of that, he knew his shit. Knew which teams would be in need of a back-up goalie at the end of the season. Knew that the chances of getting a call were lower for him, but he wasn't throwing away the hope that his play throughout the remainder of his season would spark some interest.

Plus, he was genuinely looking for advice and tips on making it. And while most questions were directed to Nyberg, whose expertise in net was golden, I didn't hesitate to throw in some advice of my own on a more generic level. It was inspiring really, seeing him get excited about the prospect of the future, and reminded me how I felt before getting drafted.

Hungry and ready to learn.

It was nearly an hour later when we finally made our exit, making sure he'd gotten the most out of the sit down as he could.

"Take the highway," Nyberg said when we climbed back into the car. "It should be clearing up, and I don't want to get stuck at every stop light, especially with all this snow."

It was really coming down now, which meant the roads were going to be awful either way. And I was also of the mind to choose the lesser of two evils. "You read my mind."

Luckily, the traffic was manageable, though there were plenty of drivers who seemed to think that snow suddenly made them incapable of driving.

Like seriously? We were in Boston and it was like they'd never seen snow before.

"Wait, slow down," Nyberg said once we hit a stretch without any drivers clutching their wheels in fear. Thrown by his words, I glanced his way, only to spot what he had clearly seen. A car on the side of the road with small plumes of smoke coming from it. "Pull over and see if they need anything. It looks like they're alone."

And sure enough, as we passed by the car, I saw the seats were empty and a lone figure had managed to pop the hood. Though clearly didn't know what they were doing as they tried to wave away the smoke.

Flicking on the turn signal, I pulled over a few meters in front of them.

"Come grab me if they need help," Nyberg said, pulling his phone out from his pocket.

"What? Why me?"

"You wanted to drive, so you get to play hero and go check things out."

"Whatever," I muttered, reaching into the back seat for the toque I knew he stashed there. Pulling it over my head, I opened my door, feeling the cold blast of air on my face as I said, "you owe me."

Chapter 6

I shielded my face as best I could from the blowing snow as I turned away from my car, or sorry excuse for one, and saw someone climbing out of the vehicle in front of me. "Any chance you're with AAA?"

I'd called a couple of minutes ago and had been informed by an all-too-perky voice that it'd be at least forty-five minutes until they could get a person out here. Though one could hope.

"No, sorry," the person yelled, muffled by the weather, but their voice was deep enough for me to associate it with a man. "Do you need help?"

Shivering, I could only imagine what I looked like to those driving by. Bundled in a winter jacket that hung past my knees, a scarf wrapped multiple times around my neck, and my hair shoved underneath my hood, I could've passed as a giant marshmallow if only my coat had been white instead of navy blue. Or a roasted giant marshmallow, given the fact I was standing next to a smoking car.

But more importantly, I was a woman alone on the side of the highway after nightfall.

"I think I'm fine," I said, hoping whoever he was, he'd get the hint that I felt more comfortable waiting for roadside assistance by myself. "I—"

My next words got stuck in my throat as the man moved closer, giving me a better view of the familiar features that were like a punch to the gut. Especially his eyes, which were glazed with worry before flashing with recognition.

"D-Derrick?" My voice shook a little, whether it was due to shock or the cold, I couldn't tell.

It was hard to believe he was standing in front of me, after I'd spent the past two weeks trying my best to push our night together out of my mind. Clearly fate had decided today was the perfect day to put me through the wringer.

"Shit, Lia," he said, his worry deepening as he stopped a foot in front of me. His cheeks were flushed and wisps of black hair poked out from underneath his hat. "Are you okay?"

A moment lapsed between us as his eyes scanned over me, my brain catching up with the situation. "I'm fine," I replied, clearing my throat as I gestured backwards, "but my car isn't. Clearly."

Taking my words for what they were—the truth—some of his concern dissolved and one side of his mouth kicked upward. "Clearly."

"Yeah, I was on my way downtown to meet friends when I saw the smoke coming from the hood and I pulled over." I was rambling, I knew, but it was better than the alternative of awkward silence. "And it didn't stop when I turned the car off, so I have no idea what's going on, but as you heard, I called AAA and hopefully they can help me out when they get here."

"Do you know how long they'll be?"

"Oh—" I waved him off before crossing my arms over my chest. "—you know how it is when there's weather like this. They'll be here as soon as they can."

While he appeared to recognize my deflection of the truth, he didn't push. "Do your friends at least know you're out here?"

I bit my lip. "I may have just told them I couldn't make it out," I said. His gaze turned flat and I quickly continued, defending my actions. "I didn't want them worrying."

"Lia—"

"Is everything alright out here?" another male voice suddenly cut in, yelling through the snow. My attention flicked to the vehicle with surprise, not realizing Derrick hadn't been alone. "Do you guys need help?"

Derrick squeezed his eyes shut. "No," he replied, voice strained. "We're good."

Either the other man didn't hear him or he completely disregarded Derrick's response, because the sound of a car door slamming sliced through the wind. And from the sigh that left Derrick's lips, I figured it was the latter.

Before I could entirely understand how my luck had brought me face to face with Derrick again, suddenly the number of tall, built men standing in front of me had doubled.

"You sure?" The newcomer smirked, nudging his elbow into Derrick's side. "Because it seemed like you guys were chatting out here for a while."

"It's been like, three minutes," Derrick muttered under his breath before casting an apologetic look my way. "Lia, this is my roommate and teammate, Ryan Nyberg. Nyberg, this is Lia."

The goalie for the Knights. Of course my wreck of a car would attract two of the most idolized athletes in the city.

"Uh, hey."

Ryan's eyebrows shot up, looking between the two of us with intrigue. "How do you two know each other?"

The second a low, almost undetectable chuckle left Derrick's lips, I narrowed my eyes, watching as he tried—and failed—to disguise it as a cough. But the shadow of a grin was enough to give him away as he thought about the answer to the question. How we knew each other, as well as how well we knew each other.

"We met a few weeks back in San Francisco. We were meant to be on the same flight back to Boston before it was canceled." Not a lie, but as I replied nonchalantly, I saw a spark of something in Ryan's gaze. Whatever Derrick had told him after returning on New Year's was clearly enough for him to connect a few dots. "We barely know one another, really," I continued.

"Nothing significant, eh?" Ryan laughed, shaking his head at his teammate. "How unfortunate."

The heat I felt on my cheeks told me I should've been embarrassed by the twist of words, but I was more amused watching Derrick's reaction to the good-natured ribbing. He rolled his eyes and brought his hand up to shove Ryan's shoulder, muttering something I couldn't quite comprehend under his breath.

"Well," I said, clapping my hands together, "thanks for pulling over to check on me, but I'm fine. Really. I'll just wait in my car until AAA gets here. No problem."

Concern crept back into Derrick's features, not buying my overly chipper tone. "Will your car even turn back on? You'll freeze if you have to wait out here much longer."

"This guy's right," Ryan said. He'd dropped his happy-go-lucky persona, now equally as troubled as Derrick at the idea of leaving me to fend for myself. Which I was perfectly capable of doing, under most circumstances. "How much longer do you think you'll have to wait for help?"

I looked between the two of them, debating how to respond this time around, but I ended up going with the truth. Sighing, I said, "half an hour at this point. Probably longer."

The two men exchanged a look before Derrick spoke. "And have you eaten dinner yet?"

"No..." I trailed off, not understanding where this was going.

"Then how about this. There's a small diner off the next exit. Our treat. It'll get you out of the cold, and trust me, you'll feel a lot better about this whole situation with some food in you. Maybe even a hot chocolate."

"Um, well, I-I don't know," I replied, stunned at his suggestion. "You guys probably have plans, and—"

"We don't," Derrick said, cutting me off and elbowing Ryan.

"He's right, we don't."

They may not have had plans, but that didn't mean they hadn't been on their way home. However, as bad as I felt for appearing to need a knight in shining armor—or two—I truly didn't want to be left in this weather to freeze.

"Then sure," I resolved, releasing a bated breath. "Let's go."

The bell over the entryway jingled as I stepped inside, the two men close behind. True to their word, it had taken all of two minutes to pull back onto the highway and arrive at the diner, and the second a surge of warmth greeted me, I realized just how cold I'd been.

Rubbing my hands together, I looked around, not at a chain but a good old fashioned, hole-in-the-wall diner. There were a few booths lining one wall, short stools situated up against the front counter, and square tables filling the rest of the space. All of it decorated to transport guests back to the 70s with red and teal leather, checkered flooring, and even a milkshake machine.

Interesting. Unexpected.

"Um… I'm just going to…" I hooked my thumb towards the washroom signs near the back.

"Sure, sure," Derrick said, his hands stuffed in his pockets. "What did you want to eat? I can put in your order."

My gaze flew towards the handwritten menu hung high behind the counter, scanning the options. "A cheeseburger is fine. No pickles."

"And a hot chocolate?" he asked, the corner of his mouth hitching upward.

I smiled shyly and nodded. "Yes, please."

Not wanting to draw out the awkwardness, I scuttled my way through the diner, needing a few moments to myself to come to terms with the turn my evening had taken.

After relieving myself and washing my hands, I stood in front of the mirror and let out a slow breath. "This doesn't mean anything," I muttered to myself, my cheeks still rosy from the cold. "This is all some kind of fated fluke and he's just being nice. There's no need to be awkward, so go out there, be confident, and you'll be fine."

And while the pep talk helped, it didn't stop me from fixing my hair into a somewhat presentable ponytail before heading back out.

Either I'd taken a lot longer than I'd thought or the service here was extremely fast, because Derrick and Ryan were already seated at one of the tables, baskets of food in front of them. "Hey," I said, sliding into the open chair where my food was. "Thanks for this."

"No problem."

A tingling sense of awareness swept over my skin as I shed my coat and picked up my cheeseburger, all because of the man in front of me. The one I'd slept with.

The last time we'd seen one another, both of us had been cool and self-assured, not the clammed up bundles of awkwardness we currently resembled as we ate in silence. But sometimes sex could do that; take a good thing and make it weird.

Luckily, Ryan ended up being the perfect tension cutter. "So, Lia, what do you do when you're not stranded on the side of the road?"

My lips pulled up with mirth as I finished chewing. "I'm actually finishing up my PhD at Harvard," I admitted, and knowing I hadn't told Derrick this back in California, I wasn't surprised to see both sets of eyes widen.

"So, was it you that I saw earlier today on campus?" Derrick asked, looking almost embarrassed that the question had slipped out so quickly.

"Wait, what?" My brows creased with confusion. "You were on campus?"

"That's actually where we were coming from when we pulled over," Ryan explained. "I was talking to Harvard's goalie at the arena and this guy tagged along."

"Yeah, and I thought I saw you walking on campus, but—" He chuckled, shaking his head. "—I also thought I was seeing things."

"I mean, it could have been me," I offered. "But it was probably somebody else. I was in my office most of the afternoon working through the lab results I collected yesterday."

"What are you studying?"

"In simple terms, I'm helping with research surrounding the generation of artificial cells. Specifically looking at ways to best transplant hand-crafted DNA into them."

The look of astonishment on their faces wasn't new, as I was used to people reacting with surprise when I explained what I did.

"Damn, Red." Ryan whistled. "You're like, really smart."

I felt a flush creep up my neck as I took a sip of my drink.

"I think it's cool." Derrick smiled warmly. "You're certainly doing a lot more for the world than either of us goons."

"Hey, even us smart people need athletes to keep us entertained," I mused.

"Yes, but if I recall correctly," he drawled, hilarity gleaming in his gaze, "you're more reliant on football players for that."

Ryan's gaze snapped to mine. "What now?"

"She's more into football than hockey," Derrick said teasingly, his voice hushed as if scandalized.

"Well, we'll have to change that, won't we."

I rolled my eyes, staying quiet and finishing off my food as I let them tag team an argument for why hockey was the better sport. It was amusing really, seeing them go to bat for the game they both had worked hard at for years, but it was also kind of heartwarming. They genuinely loved the game, and their passion for it radiated off them in spades.

Though their reasoning was cut short when my cell began to ring, roadside on the line letting me know they'd be there to help within the next few minutes.

Which meant it was time to go.

"Thanks again for all this," I said from the back seat when Derrick pulled to the side of the road again. This time behind my broken-down car since the space in front had been taken up by the tow truck, idling loudly. "And it was nice to meet you Ryan."

He smiled in return. "You too."

I clambered out of the car and was greeted with a blast of cold air that nipped at my skin. Burrowing into my scarf, I waved once more to Derrick and Ryan before heading over to greet the man in the tow truck, though my steps halted when I heard a door open behind me.

"Hey, Lia, wait a minute," he called, and I turned to watch him catch up to me. "Are you sure you don't want us to wait around? Give you a ride home or anything?"

Though it was thoughtful, I shook my head. "I'm good, really."

"Then at least let me know when you get home safely."

"Uh, yeah, sure," I said, failing to sound casual and nonchalant as I pulled my phone from my pocket. In reality though, I could feel my heart beating rapidly inside my chest as he rattled off his number and I keyed it in.

Especially because, on top of gaining another contact, I could see the missed messages in my group chat with Esme and Harper. Ten of them to be exact. All likely curious and borderline frantic after my last message telling them I couldn't make it out. Though considering I barely believed what events had transpired, I needed to find the right words before explaining myself. And I would. Hopefully.

"Great," Derrick said once I tucked my phone away. Waiting a moment, he let the silence linger before taking a step backward. "Well then—" Another pause. "—take care."

There was a charge in the air, growing more intense as we parted. Or maybe I felt that way because the ball was in my court now.

"You too," I said before turning my attention to the patient tow truck driver. You too.

Chapter 7

That night, Ryan badgered me every time I checked my phone, finding it hilarious that the hours rolled by without me receiving a single message from Lia. "Incapable of closing the deal," he'd teased when I finally retired to my room, but I'd more or less let the words roll off me, unscathed.

Sure, there was a small sting being that it was the second brush off she'd given me, but by the time I awoke the next morning, my focus had shifted. There was a game tonight, an important one, and there was still a lot of preparation to be done if we wanted to win. Game film needed to be watched, workouts needed to be completed, and our morning practice needed to go without a hitch.

Which it did, and come one o'clock, my adrenaline was up as I sat down for lunch, only to glance at my phone and see a message from an unknown number.

Lia.

Thanks again for yesterday. Sorry I didn't message sooner, but my friends dropped by after I got home and stayed pretty much until I crashed

Huh. Interesting.

I didn't doubt she was telling the truth, though as wires in my brain began to cross to formulate some sort of response, my facial features betrayed my internal thoughts. Particularly as my lips pulled into a grin.

"You got porn or something on there, Wellsley?"

Orlov chuckled as he straddled the bench beside me, trying to take a glimpse at my screen.

I rolled my eyes and flipped my phone face down. "No, idiot." I surveyed the sweat-soaked clothes he still wore. "But if you could take your stink away from my food, that'd be appreciated. Don't want to lose my appetite, you know."

"This?" He raised his arms and wafted the stench around, punctuated his movements by flexing. "This is all man, baby."

"You know you reek, Orlov," Nyberg said as he joined us. "But Wellsley here probably has a creepy smile on his face because he finally got a text from his girl."

Any teammate within earshot instantly perked up.

"Girl?"

"I don't have a girl," I drawled with denial. It'd been years since my last foray into an actual relationship, and that had ended in a burst of flames. Since then, and for the foreseeable future, short and casual suited me just fine. "Nyberg's just talking out his ass."

"Oh yeah?" Nyberg challenged, lifting a brow as he reached across the table. "Then let me see your phone real quick." Reacting out of instinct, I snatched up my phone and slid it into my sweatpants pocket. Nyberg's smirk grew as the guys around us laughed. "I rest my case."

"Look, it's really nothing," I said, running my hand through my hair with light frustration. "We—" I gestured to Nyberg. "—just happened to pull over to help a woman whose car had broken down on the highway last night—"

"What heroes."

"Someone get these two a medal."

"—and we helped her out until the tow arrived," I finished, dismissing the jabs of my teammates.

"He's right," Nyberg agreed, glossing over a short recount of the previous evening before his eyes turned mischievous. "He's just leaving out the fact that the woman we helped just so happened to be the same woman he spent New Year's Eve with out in California."

I instantly regretted ever telling the guys I'd been hooking up with someone while they'd been enjoying the night at Coach's party. Not that I'd spilled every detail like a gossiping teenager, god no, but I could only take so much hassling about how shitty it must've been for me to ring in the new year alone when I'd let it slip that I hadn't been alone. But I'd left it at that.

Now though, whistles and catcalls filled the room before questions began flying my way. Was I looking for a repeat? How hot was she? Had I known she lived in Boston when we'd hooked up? Did she have any hot, single friends?

And my response? To dig into my food and stay mum.

Thankfully, when I failed to reply to their good-natured ribbing, the conversation moved on; my dating life merely a topic that faded from their minds. Or so I thought.

"So, the New Year's Eve gal lives in Boston," Brookes said, clapping me on the back as we left the lunchroom half an hour later. Despite only having been traded to the Knights last season, he'd quickly become the person I was closest with on the team after Nyberg, and had clearly pocketed away his curiosity until there weren't so many ears listening in.

My lips twitched upward. "Seems that way," I replied, not feeling the need to mention I'd already known she was a local.

"Are you seeing her again?"

I lifted a shoulder in a shrug, bringing my steps to a halt. "I don't know. I mean, sure, there's chemistry there, but I'm not looking for a relationship. She's finishing up her PhD—" His eyebrows jumped in surprise and I chuckled, rubbing the back of my neck. "Yeah, I was surprised too. But she's busy with that and you know how it is leading up to April. Every game feels more important than the last until we clinch a spot in the playoffs." I shook my head. "New Year's was great, but I don't know if anything else is in the cards to be honest."

But even as the words left my mouth, they felt forced, and I could feel my phone burning a hole in my pocket from the text I'd left unanswered.

"You're not busy 24/7, man." Turning to face me, he began backing away with his hands up in mock surrender. "And nobody said there was any harm in a date."

Knowing he was right, I mulled it over for a moment before plucking my phone out of my pocket and pulling up Lia's message.

And because I never knew what would happen if I didn't shoot my shot, I started typing.

The whole team had put their all into the sixty minutes we spent on the ice Friday and Saturday night. We'd played strong, even when it felt like Montreal and New Jersey hadn't wanted to give us an inch, and while both games were incredibly close, we'd wanted it more. And we'd gotten the wins.

Wins that had me feeling on top of the world, especially when I'd been chosen as one of the players to take part in the shootout on Friday after the regulation and overtime periods had ended in a tie. Gliding strategically toward the net, I'd aimed to the left but had flipped my shot at the open five-hole at the last second, and grinned as it sailed across the line for a goal. That luck had continued into Saturday when my slapshot had echoed off the post at the end of the third period before ricocheting into the net behind New Jersey's goalie.

I was showing the fans, and more importantly, the team management, that I knew this game. That I could win. That I could, hopefully, help in a run towards the Stanley Cup in the coming months.

They just had to keep me around long enough for that to happen.

Another perk of having played well was that it'd given Lia and I something to talk about as we kept our conversation going.

No problem. Glad you got home safe

I hadn't jumped in right away asking for a date, but had instead played it cool, not wanting to overwhelm her. Especially figuring it was still strange to her that we'd bumped into each other again in the first place. I knew it was for me.

My plan seemed to work okay though, considering she sent along another text a few hours later to wish me good luck before the game.

Good luck tonight. My friends and I might tune in during our monthly game night

Sounds like an exciting Friday night, Red. I'd suggest a competitive round of Monopoly

Didn't want to sever any friendships, so we went with Clue and Scrabble – much safer options. And congrats on the win! Nice shot at the end there

I'd only seen her text later that night, after the excitement had wound down a few notches and I was ready to crash.

I can definitely see you sweeping the board in Scrabble. And thanks, maybe it was because you were watching.

And seeing as my message had been delivered late, it wasn't surprising that I only received a reply the next morning.

Hopefully you can still make a showing tonight then, because I won't be able to catch the game tonight

I will, don't worry. Though if you're free tomorrow, I could probably give you a give play-by-play over lunch

Game day prep had kept me busy for the majority of the morning, but when I finally got a chance to check my messages, a grin slipped onto my lips.

I can do lunch

Pick you up at noon?

See you then.

Somehow, through a stroke of luck, I found an open parking spot right around the corner from the four-story brick apartment building Lia had texted me the address to. On the edge of Cambridge, she lived close enough to the university without being surrounded by the throngs of student housing, though the streets were still bustling as I stepped out into the cold.

However, I barely reached the front doors before Lia spotted me through the glass doors of the foyer and met me on the sidewalk.

"Hey," she greeted, a wide smile on her pink-stained lips. With her hair down and curled softly, she looked gorgeous. Like a bright firecracker on a bleak night. And though her jacket concealed most of her outfit, the jeans and knee-high boots she wore did wonders for her legs.

"Hey," I echoed, leaning in to kiss her cheek. Pulling back, I noticed her grin had softened and a red tint began to color her skin. "I would've come up to meet you."

She waved me off. "Oh, don't worry about it. I've was ready early, so I figured it was better to wait down here than pace the apartment. Besides—" She laughed. "—my place is a bit of a mess."

"I'm sure it's not that bad."

"It's not dirty or anything, I keep it clean," she said, correcting herself quickly. "But since I've been working on my final defense in spurts over the weekend, there are papers everywhere that I didn't have the time to try and organize."

"You like working amongst the chaos?"

"I prefer to call it organized chaos."

"Nothing wrong with that," I said, leading her back to where I'd parked. "But I will say, if you need any help, I do know quite a bit about a good defense."

"Not exactly the same thing," she mused.

I shrugged, though it was apparent I was teasing as I said, "Same word. It's just about the perspective."

She shook her head, and as we approached the truck, I lengthened my strides to get there first, making sure to open the passenger door for her.

"Thanks." Though she lifted a brow and turned to face me as she hopped into the seat. "Did you upgrade sometime in the last two days?"

"Oh, no, the SUV on Thursday was Nyberg's. This baby's all mine."

A small noise of understanding came from her lips as she settled into the seat, and once I closed the door, I jogged around the front to slide in next to her.

"So," she began as I buckled myself in and started the car, "are you going to tell me where we're going?"

"It's actually a surprise," I replied before gesturing to her knee-high boots. "And while I love those boots, they may get in the way where we're headed."

Her gaze flitted to her boots before rising back to meet mine, curiosity flooding her features. "Why?"

"You'll see," I said, not giving anything else away.

The suspicion never completely faded as I drove through town, but she let it drop. Instead, she asked more about how my game had gone last night, wanting more while the radio soft background noise. Though when I pulled into a small parking lot fifteen minutes later and killed the engine, her eyes gleamed with amusement.

"A bowling alley?"

"What?" I asked innocently. "I never said this would be a five-star lunch."

Not to say I hadn't considered taking her out for an upscale meal, but I'd squashed that idea pretty fast once I realized I wanted today to be about having fun. To be chill. Besides, hanging out in an extravagant restaurant wasn't exactly my scene, and from what I knew about Lia so far, it wasn't hers either.

"I didn't expect it to be," she replied, confirming my thoughts. "Though I will admit, I didn't see this coming."

"Maybe that was the point," I drawled.

"Well then, let's go." She laughed, opening the car door. "Though I have to admit, I don't think I've been bowling in at least ten years."

Perfect, I thought.

Only my plan to help her bowl—you know, the classic stand behind her to help guide the ball trick—crumbled to pieces once we got going.

When we sat down at our lane to change shoes, I didn't miss the shadow of a smirk that pulled at Lia's lips when she saw some of the screens were broadcasting football.

I rolled my eyes. "Not a word."

"I didn't say a thing," she replied, miming the zipping her lips action before typing our names in and setting up the first game.

Besides us and a family with young kids occupying a lane a few down from ours, it was relatively dead, so when I put in our order—a burger, medium fry, and milkshake for each of us—it was spread out across our table before we finished our first game.

Perfect for me to snack on as I sat, watching in shock while Lia's skills began to greatly improve during the second round. Releasing the ball from her hand for her final shot, it rolled out towards the right before spinning back to the center and hitting the front pin, the rest of the pins falling in succession.

"I think somebody lied about their skills considering that's your third strike this round."

Lia grinned as she sauntered over happily and plopped herself in the plastic seat next to me. "Maybe I'm just lucky." She plopped a fry in her mouth as my features shifted in disbelief. "Or maybe bowling's just a lot more about math and science than I remember."

"Or," I trailed off as I scooted closer, my arm extending across the back of her seat, "maybe I've just been bamboozled."

When she pulled her bottom lip between her teeth, my eyes dropped to track the action, and unsurprisingly, I couldn't help myself from leaning in to press my lips against hers. Lasting only a few moments, it was soft, yet hungry, her mouth moving eagerly beneath mine before I pulled back, not wanting to get carried away.

Because I could. Easily. Especially considering I already had to subtly readjust the front of my jeans as I set up another game.

"Though now that I know you can play, I'll be sure to bring my A game."

"Mhm." Lia's mouth quirked upward. "You sure you don't need my help? I can give you some tips on how to get the rotation you want."

"How about," I countered, "we both give it our all, and the loser owes the winner a kiss?"

"Sure," she agreed. "Just be ready to pay up."

"We'll see."

Yet while I gave it my best effort, and the score had definitely been closer, she'd still come out on top. And of course, my one-track mind betrayed me as flashbacks of her on top in a different setting came rushing back.

"Well, I guess it's time I got you home," I said after watching Lia do a little happy dance, noticing we'd been here for nearly three hours. "Or, if you want—" I shoved my hands into my pockets, feeling my shoulders tense slightly. Wondering if what I was about to offer was too forward. "—we could hang out at my place for a bit."

There was a prolonged pause as she straightened, composing herself while considering what I was saying. It killed me not knowing what was running through her head. If she was on the same page as me, which I hoped she was, or if she wanted this day to end with nothing more than a kiss.

Finally, just as I was about to take my words back, I saw her eyes cloud with thinly veiled yearning.

"Your place sounds good."

Chapter 8

Sundays were typically my day off.

A day to sleep in, run errands, catch up with my parents over the phone, and laze around my apartment watching television.

And apparently, a great day to make out with hot men. Or one man in particular.

Derrick.

Whereas we never got to play out my elevator fantasy back in San Francisco, there wasn't a lick of hesitation once the doors closed this time around. My back hit the wall as his lips claimed mine—so eager, so sensuous, I was surprised my legs didn't immediately turn to jelly. His tongue traced the seam of my lips, eliciting a moan from me, and when I opened for him, I fully sank into the kiss.

So much so that I forgot exactly where we were until Derrick pulled back and the doors slid open on the twentieth floor of Derrick's high-rise.

"Am I the only one who thought that went by way too fast?" I breathed.

A chuckle rumbled his chest. "No," he mused, grabbing my hand to lead me down the hall. "Though it's certainly not over. More of a to-be-continued state."

There was no ignoring the warmth that rolled down my spine, or the quiver in the pit of my stomach surely caused by lust. All anticipation on my body's part, remembering how good it'd been with him. How good it was going to be again.

And judging by the long strides he took and the ease with which he plucked his keys from his pocket and unlocked his apartment, I wasn't the only one keen for this repeat.

"Now," he said once the door closed behind us, voice low as he backed me up against it, "where were we?"

I raised up on my tiptoes, slinging my arms loosely around his neck. "I think—" I stopped a hairsbreadth away from his lips, our breath mingling. "—right about here."

My eyes fluttered shut when he leaned in, his mouth grazing mine softly. Though before we could go any further, we were interrupted by a loud bark and a soft thunder of footsteps.

Pulling back with amusement, I saw he'd clenched his eyes shut. "I'm going to go ahead and assume that wasn't you who just barked," I said teasingly.

"No. No it wasn't."

I held in a laugh, peeking around him to see a fully-grown Labrador bounding our way, paws skidding across the hardwood. "Hey, buddy," I gushed, squatting to run a hand through his golden fur. Clearly happy to see us, his tail wagged and he panted happily. "What's your name?"

"This is Scout." Derrick dropped to our level, embarrassment from having a dog interrupt us gone except for the red tint I spotted lingering on the back of his neck. "He's technically Ryan's, but I think he secretly loves me more. Ain't that right bud? Aren't you a good boy?"

I cracked a smile, watching him interact with the dog he clearly loved as if it was his own. The scene gripped my heart in a tight squeeze, spreading a warmth through me that was only intensified when Derrick turned to meet my gaze.

"You back already, man?" I heard Ryan's voice travel through the apartment and was somewhat startled. Having been so focused on getting back to Derrick's place—or more specifically, his bedroom—it momentarily slipped my mind that he didn't live alone. "What? Couldn't seal the—"

Rounding the corner from what I assumed was a hall leading to the bedrooms, Ryan stopped short—both in steps and words—when he noticed me. He had surely only heard the tail end of our conversation, thinking his roommate had returned alone. Which wasn't the case.

"What I meant to say was," he started, rubbing the back of his neck while quickly veering away from his original thought, "it's good to see you again."

A wry grin pulled at my lips and I stood. "You too."

"How was bowling?"

"Oh, it was great," I replied gleefully. "Especially considering I ended up winning both games."

"Ouch." Ryan winced playfully, laughing as he shot an amused look at his roommate. "That must've been a hit to the ego."

With a quick shoulder shrug, Derrick rose from the ground, leaving Scout to circle around his feet. "Apparently my competitive streak wasn't enough to beat her," he drawled, tossing a small smile my way before turning back to Ryan. "She won fair and square."

I bit my lip, pushing down my full elation as my eyes flitted between them; the silent conversation that stretched between the roommates not going unnoticed. What was said was anyone's guess, but I wasn't entirely stunned when Ryan headed toward the kitchen, returning seconds later with a red leash in his hand.

"Well, I think it's about time I take Scout on his walk," he declared. "A nice, long walk along the riverside. Who knows, maybe we'll even stop at one of the guys' places." He leaned down to attach the leash and ruffle Scout's fur. "Would you like that, bud?"

Ryan's question was met with a loud bark as Derrick rolled his eyes at his roommate's exaggeration.

"Then it looks like I'll be gone for an hour or two." Grabbing his jacket from the hook near the door, he threw it on before turning back to us. This whole thing was clearly entertaining to him as hilarity shone through his features. "You guys good here?"

"We'll be fine," Derrick mused.

"Good." Ryan wriggled his eyebrows suggestively. "Don't do anything I wouldn't do."

When the door closed behind him, it felt like a deafening boom, punctuating the fact the two of us were alone again.

"He's not subtle at all, is he?" I asked, trying to calm the blush I could feel spreading across my cheeks.

Derrick chuckled. "No, not normally."

As he trailed off, a prolonged silence sprawled between us, not at all helped by the foot or so of space that separated us. And with each second, we veered further into awkward territory. Making me wonder if, somehow, I was unconsciously throwing out don't touch me signals, because surely he would make a move if I wasn't, right?

Or was this him giving me the reins? Letting me be the one to stoke the sexual flames and get them burning once more.

Tick. Tock.

"This place is nice," I finally said before mentally kicking myself for such a lame conversation starter. Couldn't I have thought of anything better? Something more original? How was talking about his apartment in any way sexy?

Admittedly, though, it wasn't a lie.

The apartment was a bit of a bachelor pad, which wasn't surprising considering two single men lived here, but it did have a modern style to it. One wall had floor to ceiling glass windows and a sliding door that led to a balcony overlooking the city, the walls were painted a subtle light grey, and the hardwood floors were stained dark brown. There was a large flat screen bolted to the wall and the rest of the furniture seemed upscale, while still comfortable. The living and dining rooms were open and spacious, while most of the kitchen was closed except the pass-through, and there were presumably at least two bedrooms down the hallway.

One I was hoping to explore. And soon.

"Yeah," he replied, trailing off while his gaze arced around the apartment. It almost seemed like there was a hint of sadness that slithered its way out of the shadows as well, but I didn't feel it was my place to prod. "It's definitely nice to split the rent, and the space, especially considering we're both out of the city so much of the year."

"Right, right." I nodded, knowing I needed some other way to spin this conversation back onto a sexier track. And then it hit me. "Actually, I just remembered something."

He lifted an eyebrow. "Oh?"

See a wariness cross his face, I realized my words could've been misconstrued as a lead up to wanting to go home. Which was the last thing I wanted in that moment.

"I never collected on that kiss from back at the bowling alley."

Understanding flared in his irises, replaced in a blink with pure, untethered heat. "Is that so?" His voice was smooth and deep as he took a step toward me, eliminating the open space. Raising a hand, he slid his fingers beneath my hair and cupped the side of my neck, his thumb running softly along my jaw. "Well, I wouldn't want to deprive you of your winnings."

My breath hitched as his mouth brushed against mine, a featherlight touch so soft it felt like a whispered cue. One that told me things were about to heat up.

And when he pulled back, eyes searching my face, he found exactly what he was looking for. My libido—an open book in my expression—ready and raring to go.

We met in the middle, both of us having had enough of skirting around each other, and the kiss immediately deepened, his tongue sliding alongside mine as we each worked to pull the other's jacket off.

With that layer gone, Derrick wrapped his arms around my waist and palmed my ass, pulling me flush against him. Enough so I could feel every hard ridge of his body, making my grip on his biceps tighten in want and with need.

And damn were those biceps just as good as I remembered.

Realizing what was building between us was in no way leading to a slow or romantic time, but instead a frantic and intense craving needing to be fed, Derrick took the lead. Without breaking the kiss, he bent down slightly, gripping my thighs and guiding my legs around his waist while walking purposefully toward his bedroom.

There was no time to close the door as he marched straight for the bed, the two of us tumbling onto the mattress in a tangle of limbs.

"I think I forgot to tell you how gorgeous you look today," he said, whispering against my throat as his lips began tracing a path down my body. "How much I love this blouse." He popped the top buttons open with ease, exposing the lacy blue bra I'd worn for just this occasion. "And how much I'd love to rip it off."

Cupping both his cheeks in my hands, I yanked his lips back to mine. "Permission granted."

A shiver danced across my skin as a husky chuckle escaped him, and it wasn't just my blouse that was stripped off. In the moments that followed, our hands were desperate, pulling at every bit of clothing between us until they were scattered across his room and we were skin to skin.

Leaning over me, his lips slowed to a torturous pace, making every nerve ending in body scream for more. "Derrick," I whined in desperation and his bark of laughter pierced through the haze of lust.

Moving his attention southward, his palms coasted across my breasts, over my stomach, and down between my legs, searing a trail along my skin as his mouth followed in quick pursuit. When he hit his destination, stroking his tongue along my center, my hips all but leaped from the bed, wanting anything and everything Derrick was willing to give. My hands gripped the sheet beneath me as he added his fingers into the mix, drawing out noises I couldn't fathom while my muscles began to tighten in anticipation.

But before I could reach my peak, he pulled away, leaving me frustrated and breathing heavily on the bed with heavy eyes and what was sure to be wild hair.

Though before I could ask why, he flipped me over with the speed and finesse of a hockey player. Hearing the telltale rip of a condom wrapper, I bit my lip, moving with him as he situated himself behind me and propped me up on my knees.

"This okay?" he rasped, gripping my hips in his strong hands to line himself up.

"Y-yes," I replied. "Please."

Needing no further encouragement, he filled me in one smooth motion, pushing all the way to the hilt before pulling back. Then he did it again, over and over in a rhythm that drove me mad. There was nothing sweet about it; it was hard, raw, and rushed. Only made better when I rose up on my elbows and moved along with him, improving the angle so he hit just the right spot.

I knew I wouldn't last much longer, but when he dropped one hand from my hip and applied the pressure I needed to my clit, I was a goner. Whimpering, I let wave after wave of pleasure wash over me, my heart pounding in ecstasy, but it didn't stop there. Derrick, yet to finish, picked up the pace, leaning over me to place wet, messy kisses along my spine. The sensation was almost too much for my languid limbs, and when I finally felt him shudder through his own climax, the two of us collapsed together on the bed, absolutely spent.

"So," he started after a stretched silence, still breathing hard, "how was that for a first place prize?"

Concealing my grin in one of his pillows, I mumbled my reply.

"Sorry, what was that?" His fingers brushed against my ribs, causing me to squirm and giggle. "I didn't quite hear you."

Cheeks flushed, I turned my head, not hiding the fact I was ogling his naked body before meeting his eyes. "Worth it."

Definitely worth it.

Chapter 9

Sleep came far too easy that night.

Derrick had driven me home before Ryan returned, which I was grateful for, seeing as I hadn't particularly looked forward to blushing as red as a firetruck under what would surely have been a knowing grin. Though when he pulled up outside my apartment, we'd spent another couple of minutes making out, hoping passersby didn't look too closely through his windows.

When I finally stepped inside, both exhausted and spilling with euphoria, I knew there was no use trying to be productive. I changed into my pajamas, tossed a bowl of leftovers into the microwave for a late dinner, and collapsed on the couch with a reality tv show on. And later, when I more or less melted into bed, my body still singing in satisfaction, I drifted off with a silly smile on my lips.

And there was no tampering the good mood I woke up with.

Not when one of my contacts fell down the sink, forcing me to wear my glasses for the day. Not when—thanks to the cold—my car wouldn't start, making me bundle up in extra layers to walk to meet my friends for our weekly Monday morning hang out. Not when the barista behind the counter told me they were out of blueberry muffins, recommending I go with their lemon poppy seed instead. And not even when I joined Esme and Harper at our usual table, and they tried to drag every last detail of the date from me.

"Tell me you guys banged." Esme watched me eagerly, impatient for a response as she turned to her own girlfriend. "She did, right?" She looked back at me, examining my features closely. "Please tell me you did."

Harper's irises sparkled with amusement. "Considering she's not denying anything, I'm assuming the answer is yes. She did."

"How about we talk about anything else?" I drawled, though I wasn't really all that bothered. They were my best friends, and if you couldn't tell your best girl friends about your Sunday sexcapades, who could you tell?

"We will, as soon as you give us something about your date," Esme countered. "Any small detail. Or big details, like how big was his—"

"Or," Harper cut her off with a bemused smile as I felt my cheeks heat, "you can just tell us where he took you."

"We went bowling."

There was a moment of silence as my response registered with them before they both burst into laughter.

"And how did that go?" Harper asked, eyes twinkling with mirth. "Did you swindle him out of house and home?"

A light laugh escaped me as I shook my head. "Not quite." Dropping my gaze, I cupped my hands around my to-go cup. "But we did go back to his place after."

Esme leaned forward in her seat, eager for the admission to come. "And…?"

"And—" I leaned in as well, dropping my voice to just above a whisper. "—we hooked up."

The squeal that followed was enough to shock me back to my side of the table, my eyes widening and face reddening as a slew of looks—both curious and annoyed—were shot our way.

"I knew it," Esme said, slapping the table loudly, not caring she had drawn in so much attention. "You just have that glow about you. A I-had-bomb-ass-sex-last-night kind of look."

"Let everyone know, why don't you?" I mumbled, shaking my head so that my hair created a make-shift wall, shielding my face from view.

"What?" Esme shrugged, taking a sip of her sugar-filled frappe. "It's nothing to be embarrassed about."

"I'm not embarrassed," I countered. At least not for having sex with Derrick again. That had been a great decision. The fact she was trying to blurt that out to the world, however, was a little embarrassing. Checking the time quickly, I continued. "But I am late." I cast a pleading look toward Harper. "Any chance I could get a ride to campus?"

"More car trouble?"

"Is it really that surprising at this point?"

"No, not really. Though this does mean you'll have to put up with this one's—" Harper hooked a thumb toward her girlfriend as we gathered our things. "—interrogation a while longer."

The corner of my lip ticked upward. "I guess I could grin and bear it."

And while she did indeed try to pester me for more details, I kept my lips sealed. Not every romp between the sheets needed to be revisited in a play-by-play break down, and honestly, I wouldn't even know where to begin if I tried. How did I put into words the kind of tension and animalistic need he seemed to bring out of me?

Impossible, that's what it was. Or at least for the time being. The last thing I needed was to be reliving these thoughts—of tangled limbs and sweaty bodies moving in tandem—while on campus.

That wasn't to say that my good mood went unnoticed, however. In fact, for a Monday morning at a university, my cheery attitude had me sticking out like a sore thumb. Professor Klein was quick to notice in our morning meeting, pointing out that I looked like I'd had a good weekend. Like I was refreshed and ready to work.

And when Miles popped into our shared office after he finished his morning class, he didn't fail to pick up on it either. Likely because I'd been humming as I made progress with my defense.

"Morning."

Grabbing my mug, already half-empty with my second cup of coffee that day, I spun around in my chair to face him. "Morning," I chirped in an echo.

He chuckled. "What's got you so happy?" His eyes drifted to the screens on my desk, my report and various data documents scattering the screen. "Did you finish the first draft of your report already?"

Snorting, I shook my head. "I'm organized, Miles, but I'm not Wonder Woman."

"Then what is it?" he asked, taking a seat in his own chair. "Did you have a breakthrough? Walk a student through a problem? Land a position with the university?"

That last one hit a bit close to home, being that there was definitely talk within the department that a lecturing spot was opening up earlier than expected. In the summer rather than the fall. Which meant if I wanted to apply, and I did, I needed to start thinking about that on top of my research, as well as pluck up the courage to talk to Professor Klein about it.

"No," I replied, shaking those thoughts from my head. For the rest of the month I'd focus on getting as much work done on my defense as I could, and hopefully, by the time a job posting went live in the coming weeks, I'd have time to dedicate to an application. "I just had a good weekend is all." He quirked a brow as a smile bloomed on my lips. "I had a date yesterday, and you know, it went well."

"Oh," he said, voice flattening as he crossed his arms over his chest. "Anyone I know?"

Thrown slightly by the apathy of his response, my forehead creased. "Uh, no, I don't think so." I paused before letting Derrick's name slip through my lips, not wanting to seem like I was bragging. But Miles and I were friends, and I didn't see an issue with telling him. It wasn't like he would blab it around town. "Unless you know Derrick Wellsley."

Without much thought, he began to shake his head, only to freeze with wide eyes seconds later. "The hockey player?"

I bit my lip and nodded. "Mhm."

"You're dating a professional hockey player?"

"I mean, I wouldn't call it dating exactly," I said, tucking my hair back behind my ear. "It was one date. Nothing serious."

Those two words were like a bolt of lightning for Miles, his expression immediately perking up. "Ah, gotcha," he replied with understanding. As though he took it to mean there wouldn't be another date, and that made him happy.

And to be fair, I didn't know if there would be another date. I had Derrick's number and he had mine, but we were both so busy, who knew what would or wouldn't happen?

Thrown slightly by his reaction, I didn't particularly want to go into any more detail on my end. And coupled with the small voice in my head whispering it was because he was actually interested in being more than friends, I felt the need to steer the conversation back toward a safer ground—our research.

After all, that was where my focus needed to be.

"Now, do I go white or red tonight?" Harper asked out loud, standing in front of her fridge, the door open as she surveyed the two bottles of wine.

"You could always jump ship," I suggested, holding up my own glass of rosé and pointing to the bottle I'd brought over. "Feel free to pour yourself a glass."

Her nose scrunched up in disgust. "No thanks," she replied, making me laugh.

The perfect pick me up after a dreadfully long week.

While most of the week had progressed normally with no real changes to my routine, I'd walked into the office on Thursday after class to see a note from Miles stuck to my computer screen. He'd found an error I'd made in my recent set of calculations, causing a handful of fully functioning genomes to appear to have small abnormalities and be unfit for further testing. And though grateful for the extra set of eyes, I couldn't fathom how I'd made that kind of mistake in the first place. I knew better, and yet I lost a full day in the lab, having to painstakingly rework my equations and rerun the simulations until I was sure the problem had been eradicated.

Thankfully, it had been, and after putting in additional hours this morning and afternoon to catch up, I'd given into Esme and Harper's messages, convincing me to come over for a Saturday wine night.

Which, funnily enough, would accompany their watch party for tonight's Knights' game.

"How about you go white and I go red?" Esme offered, cozying up next to her girlfriend before throwing a wicked smile my way. "I'm in the mood for something rich to accompany the teasing remarks that'll leave my mouth watching Lia's boy toy skate around all night."

"Boy toy? Really?"

I knew there'd be no way of avoiding the obvious elephant in the room while watching the game, but I hadn't expected the jibes to start this early. Especially because I'd already clued them in to the fact there'd been no progression on the Derrick front this week.

The team had been traveling, and other than a few miscellaneous texts conversations, there was no news to share on my end.

"What?" Esme replied innocently. "You have fun with him and—"

The loud sound of a phone ringing cut her off.

"It's not mine," Harper said, nodding to her phone on the counter as she grabbed the white wine from the fridge.

Feeling the accompanying vibrations in my back pocket, I lifted my hips off the couch to pull my phone out. "It's me," I said, only to freeze momentarily when I saw the name on the screen.

Which did not go unnoticed by Esme, as her lips turned into a knowing smirk. "Speak of the devil."

I felt the heat of a light blush rise on my cheeks, waving at them to be quiet before accepting the call. "Hello."

"Hey, how's it going?" Derrick asked, his voice rough through the phone.

"Good," I replied, running my free hand through my hair, a nervous tick despite him not being able to see me. My friend could, however, and when I flitted my gaze their way, they were watching me with amusement. "I managed to get a decent amount of my final report mapped out, so now I'm taking the night off."

"Any chance a hockey game is on your schedule for tonight?"

"Funnily enough, it is," I drawled. "And shouldn't you be getting ready? You know, smack talk, team squats, visualizing a win; all that fun stuff."

The responding chuckle shot down the line, causing a spark of tension to coil in my chest, only to be eradicated when my friends began upping their teasing. Mocking heart eyes, kissy faces, and an overexaggerated faint in which Esme fell back into Harper's arms that had me rolling my eyes.

"That's not exactly my normal ritual," he mused, "but I should get back to pregame warm-ups. I just wanted to see if you'd be interested in a ticket tonight?"

His offer put me on the spot, considering the plan tonight had been to watch and cheer from afar. The television was already on, though it was muted, with the broadcasters analyzing tonight's games and putting together their predictions. And when I finally broke the silence, all that came from my mouth were incoherent mumbles.

Thankfully, Derrick cut back in, taking the pressure off me.

"There's no strings, Lia," he affirmed softly. "We all get tickets to the games, and it's rare I put mine to use. So, if you wanted one, I could put it at the will call window for you."

"Uh, yeah, thank you," I said, still shocked at the turn of events. Though when I glanced back at my friends, who were now watching with interest, I bit my lip sheepishly. "Actually, do you happen to have two more?"

"I'm sure I can pull something together."

I grinned, watching as Esme and Harper's eyes widened. "Then great, we'll be there."

Albeit, we'd be late.

After downing the wine we'd already poured, scouring the apartment for Knights' apparel, and ordering an Uber, the puck had already been dropped. Though with less traffic than expected, we walked into the arena with five minutes left in the first period.

"You know," Esme started as the three of us wedged and twisted our way passed a row full of hockey fans to get to our seats, "I'm sorry for any teasing comments I made about you dating a hockey player. If this is one of the perks we get by association, I'm all for it."

"Would you hush?" I said, looking around surreptitiously to make sure nobody had heard her. Luckily, they all seemed to be engrossed in the game, or more specifically, cheering for Nyberg after he smothered a slap shot from the blue line. "The last thing I need right now is to be tossed into the gossip columns."

And while I could've reiterated the fact that Derrick and I were, in fact, not dating, I couldn't confidently say that was true anymore. After all, I'd agreed to come to tonight—which could, you know, possibly count as a second date if I saw him after the game—and there was no way we could backpedal into friendship territory. Not with the chemistry that seemed to ignite between us whenever we were in the same room.

So maybe, just maybe, we were dating. Casually.

And maybe I was okay with that.

Chapter 10

Every hockey player lived for the thrill of game days, and I was no different. Since I was old enough to understand the rules and how to get the crowd cheering, there'd always been a familiar thrum in my chest when I stepped out onto the ice. A sense of familiarity and adrenaline—the combination of which got me pumped up and raring to go.

Once the whistle sounded, nothing else mattered except finding a way to get the puck in the other team's net.

Though Tampa's defense certainly weren't letting that happen easily.

"We got this," Coach said in the locker room after the first period ended without a single goal. "We're playing fast and getting our shots off, so keep it up. Find ways to get through their defense, because while they're strong, we're stronger."

"Hell yeah, we are!"

Coach chuckled proudly at Orlov's outburst. "I expect all of you to have that kind of determination going back out there, because we need it. It's not enough to avoid mistakes. I need each one of you to give it your all. To step up and leave everything you have out on the ice. And if you do that, I have no doubt we'll walk away with a win."

"Knights on three!" Simmons shouted, rousing the team as we headed back out.

"One, two, three, Knights!"

Returning to the game, I couldn't get Coach's words out of my head. They were cemented there, playing on repeat each time I jumped over the boards to join the action. And while that didn't magically make things easier, it did help my focus. I could sense the moves the defensemen would make before they made them, I was keyed in to where my teammates were on the ice and where I needed to be, and I let the noise of the crowd sink into the background, fixated solely on one thing.

Scoring.

And I thought I had the perfect opportunity after dekeing out a Tampa skater and circling the back of the net. But the goalie had me beat. If I would've let the shot off, I knew he would've buried it, so instead of killing the play in search of my own glory, I quickly passed the puck to Brookes. Ready and waiting on the other side of the net, his one-timer sailed cleanly into the back of the net before the Tampa goalie could even slide over and try to stop it.

With the lamp lit up, the arena erupted—cheers from the fans and music from the DJ booth—as I joined the guys in celebration. But only for a moment.

Because we all knew one goal was nothing in hockey, especially in a hard-fought game.

As the minutes of play time ticked down, it was clear to both sides that this would indeed be a nail biter. Back and forth we went, moving the puck up and down the ice. Shoving Tampa up against the boards to keep the momentum on our side as much as possible.

But something inside me still burned. A familiar feeling that came around once and a while that told me this was my game. My show.

And my time came when there were only two minutes left in the game.

Brookes, Schmidt, and I were moving the puck around Tampa's end, trying to find an opening as the goalie's eyes followed our every move while also trying to run down the clock. But after so many passes, I just felt it.

That urge to shoot.

So, when the puck landed back on my stick, I lunged forward and aimed a missile straight for the top right corner of the net.

Only to see it sneak passed the goalie's blocker and land beautifully in the net.

Throwing my hands up in celebration as my teammates on the ice huddled around me, I felt a pressure lift off my chest, knowing this game was ours. And as I took my seat on the bench, chugging water as our third line took care of the rest of the clock, exhilaration coursed through my veins.

Especially when the final whistle blew and I saw my face on the jumbotron, having been named the top player of the game, with Brookes and Nyberg number two and three.

"That's what I call a game, boys!" Simmons roared as we all crowded into the locker room, prompting another round of hoots and hollers from everyone.

It was like this after every win, no matter if it was a home or away game, because by tomorrow, our minds needed to be zeroed in on the next objective. The next game. There was no time to revel in the success.

But boy did I want to.

"Damn, man, you were on fire tonight," Nyberg said clapping my shoulder after shedding his gloves and head gear.

"So were you, dude. Nice shutout."

"Thanks." His grin turned knowing as he wiggled his eyebrows suggestively. "But admit it, you were trying to show off for your girl in the stands, weren't you?"

I rolled my eyes, because honestly, while I'd known she was in attendance, my performance hadn't been for her benefit. It'd been for me.

My agent had called earlier this morning to clue me in to the fact that the higher ups were still throwing my name around for a possible trade. So, tonight I'd given it my all. To prove to myself, and to the front office, that I belonged here. That I was a Knight.

"Did I hear that right?" Brookes joked, cutting in and nudging my other side. "Wellsley's got a good luck charm in the stands?"

"Well thank fuck for that," another teammate said with a chuckle. "You were a rocket tonight, man."

"He certainly was," Coach said, coming up behind me. I turned and grinned at him. "And no matter the reason, you've scored yourself a date with the reporters tonight, son. Hurry and change, because they're expecting you in less than five." His gaze flickered to Nyberg. "You too. You'll be up after him."

"Yes, Coach."

"See you both in there."

As he retreated, I began shedding the rest of my gear, but because I knew I wouldn't have time to shower, instead of changing back into my suit, I threw on a spare t-shirt and pair of sweatpants I had in my locker.

"Well, as much as I'd love to sit here and listen to you all rag on me for inviting a friend—"

"A girl friend," Brookes emphasized.

"A friend," I repeated, "to the game, I'm needed elsewhere."

"Kill it out there Wellsley," someone shouted to my back as I headed for the door, and I pumped my fist in the air three times, excitement still running through me.

I could do this. I'd done it before on a few occasions. It was no big deal.

And luckily, when I sat down in front of the single microphone on stage, looking out at the rows of reporters, the questions that came my way were easy to answer. Because the answers were true.

Were me and my teammates under pressure after that first goal to maintain our lead? Of course we were. There was always pressure to pull out a win, especially the further into the season we got.

How was my shoulder after the hard hit I took into the boards in the second? It was good. Nothing to worry about. Hockey players knew how to take hits, and I was no different.

For my goal, did I see an opening, or did I shoot blindly and hope it went in? In the position the Knights were in, I knew it wouldn't be smart to just shoot the puck at the net. We didn't want to give Tampa the chance to grab the rebound, head to the other end of the ice, pull their goalie, and score. So when I saw the opening on the ice, I aimed for the top right corner, knowing that would be the hardest place to protect in the stance Tampa's goalie was in.

How did it feel to be a part of both the goals tonight? Absolutely amazing.

I was smiling and laughing with the reporters, getting ready to wrap things up and let Nyberg take the hot seat—though one reporter decided to take things in a different direction.

"Rohan Basak with the Score. Can you confirm or deny the rumor that the Knights are looking to trade you and bring in a prime enforcer for the team?"

His question was like a punch to the stomach; his words like a bucket of ice water falling over me. I flinched, then froze, my mind scrambling for some semblance of a reply, but nothing came. Instead, silence overtook the room, everyone watching as the metaphorical pedestal I'd been on was ripped away, leaving me to tumble.

"Sorry, but he won't be addressing any trade rumors today, as that is all they are: rumors," the team publicist said, saving my ass. She motioned for me to head back to the locker room, and I nodded numbly, following her orders. "We'll now be bringing out Ryan Nyberg to answer the final questions for the night."

The swift change of subject didn't do much to distract the reporters from my stiff shoulders, however, as I felt the weight of their stares on my back as I left the room.

"Hey," Nyberg said, putting his hand on my arm as I went to pass by him. Flicking my gaze up to meet his, I saw the worry creasing his forehead. "You okay?"

"Yeah," I replied, though it wasn't the truth. More of an automated response.

Which he seemed to recognize, uncertainty clouding his eyes, but he didn't push. "Okay," he trailed off, "but if you want to talk, let me know, because that guy's question was utter bullshit."

"He's right, boy," Coach said. Having been standing off to the side, he moved closer as Nyberg left to face the masses. "Don't let reporters get inside your head, because they don't know the full story. And while I can say I don't want to see you get traded, sometimes that's just the way this league works." Lifting his hand, he rested it on my shoulder in support. "But nothing is set in stone yet, so focus on the things you can control. Your attitude and your game. You played great tonight, and you deserve to celebrate, just make sure to be back at the arena tomorrow morning ready to put in the work all over again."

I nodded in response. "Yes, sir."

Except the will to celebrate that had been raging inside my chest just minutes before had been doused, with only a few flickering flames remaining. And those only sparked after I noticed a text from Lia when I returned to the locker room.

Great game tonight! Congrats on the goal and the assist.

I couldn't help the small grin that pulled at my lips, kicking my mood up marginally despite the overwhelming gloom and doom in my head. Though I guess if I had to save face and celebrate, doing so with Lia at my side felt like the best option.

Thanks, babe. Any chance you're still hanging around?

We're a few streets over at a local pub, why?

Any chance it's Apollo's?

It is.

That's the bar me and the guys usually hit up after games… you up for a little extra company?

Extra company always welcome. See you soon.

Apollo's was pretty packed when we strolled in twenty minutes later. Tables were packed, the pool tables were in use, and while one of the TVs was broadcasting a late-night game between Dallas and Calgary, the rest were showing highlights from our game.

Prompting enough of the patrons to notice our presence, though given we were regulars at this point, there was no special treatment. Fans threw out congratulatory sentiments—like good game and nice goal—but nobody went out of their way to fuss over us, and we all appreciated it.

Especially me, because while hockey was the main constant in my life, and something I loved with every inch of my being, I really did not want to talk much hockey tonight. I didn't want to revel in the game, knowing that if this trade talk wasn't just a rumor, it could be one of my last wins in navy and silver. I wanted to forget, and with that in mind, I turned my eyes to the crowd and immediately spotted the redhead I'd been looking for.

"Hey, guys, Lia's here, so I'll catch up with you all later," I said, moving to split off from them while most of them headed for the bar.

Schmidt looked at me like I was crazy. "Come on, you're the man of the night and you're not going to drink with us?"

"Let him go have his fun. He's earned it," Nyberg cut in teasingly, though he threw me a look of acknowledgement. He hadn't mentioned the reporter crap to anyone else on the team, but had realized that it'd thrown me off, and I was thankful for him trying to cover for my shitty mood.

"What? Don't want to introduce us to your girl?" Orlov teased, nudging me with his elbow. His gaze swept around the bar. "Which one is she?"

I rolled my eyes, motioning to where she sat with her friends. "The redhead near the back."

"Damn."

I smacked the side of his head lightly. "Shut up, asshat."

He chuckled. "So, I'm guessing you need to keep her to yourself so that she doesn't come over here and realize we're all much better catches than you?"

"More like so she doesn't have to question why I hang out with you all off the ice," I corrected, running my hand through my hair. "Plus, like I said before, it's nothing serious. We're just having a bit of fun."

"Well, if your fun heads back to the apartment, let me know," Nyberg said, lowering his voice as he clapped me on the shoulder. "I'll find somewhere else to crash."

I lifted a brow. "Yeah?"

"Of course." He smirked. "I've already got my eye on the pretty little blonde at the end of the bar."

And sure enough, when I glanced in that direction, the same blonde was looking our way and checking him out.

"Then I'll be sure to give you a heads up when we leave," I mused before finally weaving my way through the crowd.

Coming up behind Lia's chair, I saw one of her friend's eyes widen as she spotted me. Using all the strength I could muster, I plastered a smile on my lips. "Hey."

Lia leaned her head back to meet my eyes and grinned, reaching for my hand. "Hey, we were just talking about you."

"All good things I hope?"

"You'll never know, now will you?"

I hoped none of them caught the half-heartedness of the laugh that escaped me as I said, "I guess not." And to further distract from the fact, I turned to greet her friends. "I'm guessing the two extra tickets tonight went to you two?"

"They did," the woman with shoulder-length brown hair said, "and thanks for that. Being in the arena was ten times better than watching the game from our living room."

"A live hockey game always takes the cake in my books," I commented. "Though I may be a little biased."

The three women laughed, and when they began to quiet, I felt Lia's hand squeeze mine. "Derrick, this is Esme—" Lia pointed to the woman with a pink pixie cut first before moving over to the brunette. "—and Harper. And you guys already know this is Derrick."

"Sure do," Esme replied with a wide grin.

"Well, it's nice to meet you guys." I looked down at the table to see most of the glasses were nearly empty. "Did you all want another round? My treat."

"I'll come with," Lia said as her friends nodded and began to rattle off their orders. "You'll need an extra set of hands to carry everything back."

Not dropping my hand, she began pulling me in the direction of the bar, but after only a few steps, I leaned closer to her. "You sure this isn't just some ploy to get me alone," I teased, my teeth scraping the edge of her ear to cause a visible shiver.

Stopping next to a pillar, she took a step backwards, leaning up against it. "And if it is?"

"Well," I said, stepping closer, my eyes dropping to her lips, "how do you feel about PDA?"

So far, all of our kisses had been behind closed doors or away from prying eyes, and before planting one on her in front of everyone, I wanted to make sure she was comfortable with that.

And by the way she stood on her toes, cupped my cheeks, and closed the remaining distance between us, I figured she was.

Molding my mouth to hers, I gripped her hips, more than appreciative of her curves as she parted her lips, inviting me in deeper. As our tongues tangled, I felt a rush of heat sweep through my veins, wanting this to last a whole lot longer than a handful of moments.

Especially when she began to pull back, a small hum of excitement falling from her lips.

"I wanted to do that after you scored tonight, but better late than never, right?"

"Totally," I agreed, pecking her lips once more.

She grinned as her hands trailed down my arms, intertwining with my own when she reached them. "But really, I know I already texted you, but the game was awesome. You played great."

"Damn right I did."

And management needed to recognize that.

The thought was immediate, killing off any vibe our kiss had created as it popped into my head without any prompting. Unsurprising given the festering anger after the press conference, but it was true. I was a Knight, had been for years, and I wanted to stay in this city. I wanted to stay with this team, and I'd do anything in my power to do so.

The heartbreaking thing, however, was I didn't know if it would be enough.

Chapter 11

When I opened my eyes, it was immediately obvious I wasn't in my own bedroom. For one, the blackout curtains succeeded in blocking out the early morning sun, whereas my cheap set of blinds would've had the room pouring with light. Secondly, there was a digital clock with large red letters staring back at me that I certainly didn't own. Then there was the hockey equipment pushed into the corner, and to top it off, the pillows and sheets—and let's be honest, the entire room—smelt like Derrick.

Far from overpowering or off-putting, it was fresh and intoxicating. A subtle mix of pine and citrus that had me turning my nose into the cotton and inhaling deeply. Only to exhale slowly as I was brought back to how I'd ended up here.

Being in the stands for the game had been unexpected, especially on a night I'd promised to spend with the girls, but the fact that Derrick had been open to extending an invite to them had made it impossible to say no. After all, Esme and Harper might have revoked my friendship card if I had. And even though we'd been to a handful of games over the years, there was something different about being in the middle of the pumped up crowd, watching everyone on the edge of their seats, ready to cheer for someone I knew. There was an added level exhilaration—even more so when that person ended up being the star of the show.

Derrick had rocked it out on the ice last night, his goal and assist propelling the team to a hard-fought win, yet after it all, he'd chosen to celebrate with me. My friends hadn't been able to stop directing sly, knowing looks my way as the four of us sat at the table in the back of the bar, Derrick more or less ignoring the rest of his teammates to spend time with us. And while it'd certainly had me feeling giddy and affectionate as the night wore on, it also left me feeling a bit confused.

This 'thing' between us was meant to be casual, and on my side, it was. I had no delusions of grandeur. We got on great, and yes, the chemistry was off the charts, but to actually be together? In a relationship? I couldn't see how two incredibly busy and career-focused people could make something work.

It was a have-fun-while-it-lasts type connection, but last night, I'd be lying if I said there wasn't a voice in the back of my head that Derrick was possibly beginning to think of it as something more.

Hence the confusion.

Though it hadn't altered how the night ended.

Which led to where I was now: sprawled beside him in bed, my clothes strewn across the room, and feeling satisfied after another night together. Admittedly, very similar to that first morning back in San Francisco. Except this time, the urge to sneak away before he woke up was nowhere to be found.

I was, however, debating whether or not to get up and scour the apartment for a cup of coffee when there was a shift from the other side of the bed and a muscular arm snaked its way around my bare waist.

"Good morning," Derrick mumbled, nuzzling his nose into the back of my neck.

I giggled in response and squirmed, unconsciously rubbing my naked body against his. So it was no surprise when I felt his erection prodding against my ass cheek. "Definitely feels like a good morning."

"Of course it is, especially because you're still here this time."

My cheeks flushed as I rolled over and while I didn't expect to see it, I was relieved not to see an ounce of anger or animosity in his features. Instead, his expression matched the playfulness of his words as his hand on my waist coasted upward to my breast. "Did I ever apologize for sneaking out that morning?" I asked sheepishly.

His eyes, though tired, gleamed. "I don't remember receiving a formal apology, no."

"Well—" I leaned forward and, despite what was sure to be a bad case of morning breath, captured his lips with my own. The kiss was tender, yet urgent as he allowed me to take the lead. Cupping the side of his face, I nipped at his bottom lip, following up with a quick sweep of my tongue. And when I arched against him suggestively, he couldn't take it any longer. Moaning against my mouth, he pulled me closer and devoured my mouth until I pulled back a minute later, panting with a pleased smile "—how was that?"

"Damn good," he replied, giving me another quick kiss. "But," he continued trailing kisses down my neck and along my collarbone, "I can think of something even better."

I shivered as his teeth scraped gently against my shoulder and his grip tightened on my thigh, propping it up and over his hip. The hard ridge of his cock was now very prominently between my legs, and every nerve ending in my body was suddenly hyper focused on Derrick. The muscles in his thighs, the hard ridges of his abs, and the way his fingertips slowly dragged down the front of my body before dipping between my thighs.

"Don't you have practice this morning?" I mumbled against his lips as he brought them back to mine. He made a dismissive grunt and I laughed, allowing his tongue to tangle with mine for a moment before pulling back once more. "No really." I giggled, turning my head towards the pillow to avoid his lips. "Don't you have to get ready?"

He sighed, knowing I was right when he glanced over me to see that the clock read eight thirty. "I do," he admitted, "but I could really use some company in the shower." His eyebrow quirked suggestively when I peeked up from the pillow. "You know, somebody to wash my back and all that."

"Well, if it'll help you get to practice on time, how can I say no?"

A victory growl left his mouth and suddenly we were on the move. Gripping me tightly to him, he rolled over and stood, marching purposefully toward the bathroom as my arms and legs wrapped around his enormous frame. Stopping only to grab a condom from his dresser, he didn't put me down until he'd thrown open the shower curtain, turned on the spray, and brought us both underneath the water stream.

The water was a shock to the system, but as my feet hit the ground, I was immediately distracted by Derrick's mouth when it claimed mine once more. There was no tenderness this time around, just pure hunger and desire, our lips moving sloppily against each other under the spray. And then his lips were gone, replaced by the sound of the condom being torn open. There was a brief interlude as he rolled it on, but then he lined up and pushed forward, filling me in one smooth thrust.

I clung to his shoulders, my nails surely digging into his skin, but all I could think about was finding the right groove. His hips jerked time and time again, and while the sensation sent a jolt of pleasure through my veins each time, it wasn't anywhere near the level I needed it to be.

"Need a different angle," I said, my lips sliding against the skin of his neck.

There was no hesitation on his end as he said, "you got it," and pulled out, only to immediately turn me around to face the wall. "Put your left foot up on the edge of the tub," he growled into my ear, and after following his instructions, I felt him grip my hips and slowly slide back inside me. "Better?"

I moaned and circled my hips, which he took as a good sign before beginning to thrust hard and deep. Over and over again. And just when I was about to say I needed some other kind of friction to get me there, one of his hands moved down to the place where we joined to give me the direct pressure I needed. "Yes," I said, leaning my head against the cool tiled wall. "That's perfect. Just... keep doing that."

"Can do."

And instead of being bothered by the water or worrying about whether or not we were about to slip, I was totally zoned in, reaching for the pleasure that was growing inside of me. Kindling turned to fire then to a blaze. My entire body clenched up when I reached the point of no return, and seconds later, a low groan left Derrick's throat as he shuddered through his own release, pumping a few final times to draw out the pleasure for both of us.

Finally, when the both of us began to come down from the high, breathing heavy, he pulled out, turning me back around to face him.

For a moment, the only thing that mattered was the identical grins we both wore, but then reality came crashing down over us. Or better yet, water did. We'd been a bit too careless finding the perfect shower sex position, and without realizing it, had accidentally pushed the shower curtain out of the way, leaving a stream of water to puddle across the rest of the bathroom.

"As much as I enjoyed that, I think the floor's almost as wet as you were," Derrick mused.

Swatting at his chest, I couldn't help but laugh as I collapsed into his arms, my legs wobbly. Because while we had indeed made a mess, there were absolutely no regrets.

Scout's nose poked into my thigh as he scampered between Derrick and I, and I ran my hand through his fur. "Ryan's not home?" I asked, suddenly very aware of what he could've seen and heard if he was.

A tiny breath of relief escaped me when Derrick shook his head. "Ninety-nine percent sure he went home with a chick he met last night," he responded. After cleaning up the bathroom, the two of us had dressed—me in my outfit from the day before and him in sweats, ready for practice—and had migrated to the kitchen. I hadn't been expecting much, but ever the gracious host, Derrick had fired up the coffee maker. He'd then quickly whipped up a pan of scrambled eggs while instructing me to make toast, and within minutes, the two of us had put together a breakfast to replace the calories we'd just burned. "Speaking of which, your friends were funny last night."

"You mean embarrassing?"

Jolted back to the four of us talking, I certainly remembered myself blushing after a few too many tales had spewed from Esme's mouth, with Harper chiming in a time or two.

Derrick shook his head, leading me over to the couch to eat. "No, they were great." He tossed a wry smile my way as the both of us situated ourselves. "Maybe a little too keen to share some stories about how you fell asleep at a hockey game a few years back," he mused, eyes twinkling, "but great nonetheless."

"In my defense," I said, jabbing my fork into my eggs, "I'd spent 10 hours in the lab that day. I was surprised I had the energy to walk up to our seats, let alone cheer for a whole period before conking out."

Chuckling, he grabbed the television remote from his coffee table and flipped the power on. "Hey, I can't fault you for cheering the team on, and if any of the other players had joined the conversation last night, I'm sure one of them would've—"

His words stopped. What I thought for a moment was a simple catch of the tongue was something much more when I noticed the blood drain from his face, his hands clench, and his gaze lock onto the television.

Where a sports newscaster spoke and eight big, menacing words took up the screen beneath him.

ROCKY ROAD AHEAD FOR THE KNIGHTS AND WELLSLEY?

"Last night, Derrick Wellsley put on a show for the crowd as he scored both a goal and an assist during the Knights' home win against Tampa. But is there friction between the man and his organization?" My eyes flickered back and forth between Derrick and the television, shocked at what I was hearing. "At last night's press conference, a reporter tried to get to the bottom of this rumor, and by the reactions of both Wellsley and the team's publicist, we think there just might be legs to this story. Take a look for yourselves."

And then a clip from the press conference began to role, showing the exact thing the sportscaster had described. A pained Derrick sitting up in front of a crowd, shell-shocked and silent, not knowing how to respond when asked about a rumored trade.

Suddenly I had a thousand questions. Had he known about the rumors? Was he fighting to stay? Hoping to go? Where had the reporter got their lead from? How could they ask something like that after Derrick had won them the game?

Then an uneasy question popped into my mind, because I had a feeling the answer was yes.

Was this whole debacle why he'd stuck close to me last night instead of his teammates?

"Derrick?" I asked, my voice quiet as the clip ended and they dove into another story. When he didn't respond, I reached over and placed my hand gently on his thigh; the touch snapping him out of it. "Derrick... are you okay?"

His forehead creased as he ran a hand through his hair, the corners of his mouth sinking into a frown. "Yeah." He paused, then shaking his head. "No. I don't know. It's complicated."

"Is what they're saying true? Are you being traded before the deadline?"

He gave me a brisk nod. "Nothing's set in stone," he replied, his voice low and eyes cast downward, "but my name's been tossed around for a trade since the end of last season."

I felt and heard the brokenness in his words. All season, through practices and games, he'd been playing—giving it all he had—for a team that didn't want to keep him. I tried to grasp at something to say. Anything that would make this situation better or turn back the clock. I came up short, however, because how did you console a man who was possibly about to have his life upheaved?

You couldn't.

The expression on his face alone pulled at every string inside my chest. His eyes—that minutes ago were bright and teasing—were now hollow. Smile erased. Pain and frustration etched into every crevice of his skin.

Silence dragged on for a few moments before, finally, he took a deep breath. Then he exhaled, defeated. "Any chance we can not talk about this and just enjoy breakfast? I've got to be out of here in less than twenty to make it to the arena on time."

In other words, no talking about serious stuff. Message received.

"Sure," I forced out, masking the part of me that wanted to help and instead pivoted the conversation to the upcoming Super Bowl.

At least he'd unknowingly reassured me that last night had been nothing more than him wanting to avoid hockey in all capacity. There were no second thoughts about the nature of our relationship on his end. This thing between us was casual.

And casual was how it'd stay.

Chapter 12

The days ticked down, flying past in a whir of traveling, strategic practices, and hard-fought games.

When it came to playing—whether that be in a scrimmage or out in front of a crowd—I was zoned in. Focused on my teammates, my opponents, the path of the puck, and doing everything I could to propel the team to victory.

It was everything else in my life that fell victim to my distracted mind. On edge, the voice in the back of my head began growing louder and louder, repeatedly reminding me that my time in Boston was likely coming an end.

After that first story had run—a dark shadow over a great performance on my end—the gossip about a possible trade had picked up steam. Now there were whole ass websites dedicated to tracking the latest sports news leaks, and everybody was wondering what the outcome would be.

No one more so than me.

I tensed every time my phone pinged with a message and could feel the stress fill my body when my agent called to check in. Now, when I walked into the Knights' complex, I felt like people had their eyes on me, watching and waiting for the perfect moment to tell me I'd been booted out. And with the speculation now out there, I'd started distancing myself from my teammates outside of the arena, except Nyberg, of course. It was just easier this way, because while most of them ignored the elephant in the room, understanding that nothing could be done to save me, it still stung whenever a look of pity or sympathy got tossed my way. Like the ink on the paper had already gone and dried.

I felt like some part of me was broken, or at the very least crumbling under the pressure of this specific spotlight. Which was why, before I climbed on the team's morning flight back to Boston, I was strolling the streets of New York, following the directions my agent had texted me to a coffee shop around the corner from our hotel.

Answers. I needed answers. And while they wouldn't be concrete, I needed some kind of footing to stand on knowing that the trade deadline was less than ten days away.

Stepping inside the coffee shop, I took a moment to shake the snow off me and arced my gaze in search of Ken. Easily finding him, I zigzagged through the growing line of customers and headed to the table he was seated at.

He stood as I approached, offering his hand to shake. "Great game last night, man. It's nice to see you giving it your all out there."

I mustered up a small smile. "Thanks," I responded as we both sat down. "And it's good to finally be able to hash all this out face to face."

Nodding in agreement, he said, "It's definitely not something I like to do over the phone, so—" I stiffened, bracing myself as he hopped right into things. "—while we don't have full confirmation, there's a high likelihood you're one of the Knights' prime pieces as they consider offers leading up to the trade deadline."

Fuck.

He certainly hadn't beaten around the bush.

A bubble of panic began to brew inside of me, but I pushed it down as best I could. I needed to have my thoughts straight for this conversation, so I took slow breaths and leaned forward, my elbows resting on the table as my hands covered my eyes.

"Then what are my options? Is there even anything I can do at this point?"

I tried to rack my brain for everything I knew about the trading process, because I wasn't a newbie to it. This was just the first time it was unwelcome on my end.

Having been drafted young, but in a late round, I'd bounced between three minor league teams the first couple years of my career before being called up to play for Pittsburgh. And while I'd done well in the games I'd suited up for, come the end of the season, I'd been sent to the Knights.

I'd been twenty-two—ripe and ready to play—and until last year, I thought I'd found the team I meshed with. The one I'd play with until I retired.

But clearly I'd been naïve about that.

Ken's expression was understanding, knowing this wasn't the path I wanted my career to take, but also professional. "Honestly, there's not much that can sway management's mind once they become dead set on acquiring new players to shake things up." The last shred of hope I'd been clinging to disappeared from reach. "But there is some good news. With the rumours going around the league that you're one of the players the Knights are willing to trade, I've received calls from a few teams to gauge your interest in the case a deal was made."

"Okay," I said, not fully hiding the dejected sigh that followed. "Which teams?"

"New Jersey, Nashville, and Los Angeles."

While Jersey was not somewhere I'd be keen to go given their losing record the last five years, Nashville wasn't half bad. L.A., however, was the surprising and intriguing option.

Having grown up in California, I'd cheered for the Los Angeles Royals and, as a kid, had imagined playing within their ranks. That was until I realized the probability of doing so was next to none.

"Los Angeles? Really?"

Ken nodded, knowing exactly why I'd perked up slightly. "They're looking to bulk up their second line, which is where you would come in. Same position in the roster, but a new home."

"And the other two? Jersey and Nashville, what are they looking for?"

"Nashville is similar to L.A., though they might bounce you between the second and third lines to find the right fit for you in the roster, but Jersey is honestly just looking for someone to give them a spark."

"Yeah, I really don't see myself in Jersey, to be honest," I said, running a hand through my hair stressfully, working through the thoughts bouncing around my head.

"I didn't think you would, but I wouldn't be doing my job if I didn't tell you that was a possibility."

"Understood, but can you let them know I'm likely not the player they're looking for? Give them something that'll hopefully sway them away from going into talks with the Knights' management?"

"Can do," Ken replied. He then raised a brow. "And Nashville and Los Angeles? How do you feel about those options?"

"Nashville is a good team, so let them know I'm open to talking. And you know I love California. If I could play for the Royals, that would be a great shot for me to play for the team I grew up cheering for. Tell them I'd be open to talking too, but in both cases, only if the Knights initiate conversations. If something falls through for some reason and the Knights change their mind, I want to stay."

While the look he gave me in return was one of certainty—one that told me I should put any hope of clinging to Boston out of my head—there was also a touch of sympathy to it. But luckily for me, he didn't stick the stake in my chest by fighting me on my request. Instead, he simply said, "I'll make the calls."

Completely opposite to my own mood, my teammates all seemed to be in the same headspace on the short flight back to Boston—rowdy and buzzing with optimism. Still riding the high from our win the night before, there were people speculating how long it'd take for us to clinch a playoff spot and others getting into a heated competition around one of the in-flight entertainment games.

Yet I sat alone, my headphones in, trying my best to tune everything out. I wasn't about to hop in and pretend like I wasn't simply waiting for the other shoe to drop in terms of where I was headed, but I also didn't want to offload my problems on my teammates.

Though I needed to talk to someone, and when I opened my messages to see the last conversation I'd had with Lia days before, I clicked it open without much of a thought.

Met with my agent before boarding. Looks like it's only a matter of time before the front office ships me off in exchange for fresh legs.

Both our schedules had been crazy busy over the last week, and while I expected a response to take a while, I was surprised to see three little dots pop up within a few seconds of the message being delivered.

I'm sorry. I can't imagine how that feels. To know it's coming, but still having to put on a brave face and play hard until it does.

Well, I can tell you it definitely doesn't feel good, that's for sure.

Honestly, I can't think of what to do or say right now, but I can offer solace in the form of pizza and movies if you wanted to swing by tonight.

Will there be pineapple on the pizza?

I promise there won't be, and you can choose the movie. I won't even complain if it's a horror.

As tempting as it would be to have you in my lap the whole film, scared out of your mind, I'm thinking more of a classic, but it doesn't really matter to me. If I swing by around seven, will you be home by then?

Seven works. And in the meantime, I suggest buying a packet of gummy worms. They always pick me up when I'm feeling down.

Will take that under advisement.

We continued texting back and forth, moving away from the serious tone I'd started with and leaning more toward lighthearted banter until the plane began to make its descent.

In the hours that followed, I was tasked with compartmentalizing my feelings to the best of my ability as everybody headed to the arena for practice. There was no way I wanted to be responsible for lowering team morale or prompting any questions as to where my head was at. Which meant putting my head down and working just as hard as I did every other day. Acting like everything was fine.

Though truthfully, I may have put a little extra energy into the checking drills, needing some kind of physical outlet for my internalized aggression.

But when the whistle blew and we were all dismissed, no-body—not a teammate or coach—had noticed anything off about me. Or if they did, like I expected Coach Davidson had, they didn't say anything.

It was only after I'd showered and changed that I figured the jig was up, when Nyberg came over to clap me on the back.

"Dude, you coming to Schmidt's for video games and beer?"

Or not.

"Uh, I don't think so," I said, pulling my phone out of my pocket to check the time. It was just past five, and while I still had nearly two hours before I was expected at Lia's, there was no way I could keep up this emotional façade for more than a few more minutes. "I already have plans."

He raised an eyebrow suspiciously. "Plans? Today?"

"Yeah, I'm heading to Lia's later."

"Wait—" His eyes bugged out. "—seriously? You've got a date planned for Valentine's Day?"

Valentine's Day. Shit. I really hoped Lia wasn't expecting tonight to be about a ridiculous holiday, because I really didn't need that kind of expectation on top of everything else right now.

I shook my head vehemently with denial. "No," I gritted out. "No, you've got it wrong. We're just ordering pizza and watching a movie or two. There's nothing special about it."

The last Valentine's Day I actually cared to celebrate had been years ago, with someone I liked nothing more than to forget these days. But it had been about flowers and chocolate, with reservations at a fancy steakhouse for dinner. Tonight was the complete opposite of that. It was chill. Casual. Not romantic at all.

"Does she know that?" Nyberg asked, looking as though he didn't believe a word I said.

And while I had no way of confirming that she did, in fact, know tonight had nothing to do with Valentine's Day; I really, truly, hoped she did.

At five minutes to seven, I pressed the buzzer to Lia's apartment and heard her voice crackle over the speaker moments later.

"Hello?"

"It's me."

"Come on up," she said, and the door to her building's lobby beeped open.

Stepping inside, I was just about to let the door close behind me when I saw a delivery man, pizza in hand, looking to follow me inside.

"Any chance that pizza is for Lia?" I asked, holding the door open for him.

"I've got two actually, but yeah, one's for Lia in apartment 406," he replied, glancing down at the receipt as the both of us headed to the elevators, stepping onto the open one waiting. "You the boyfriend?"

"Something like that," I replied, not wanting to complicate things as I fished a ten and a five out of my wallet. "Here, keep the change and I'll save you the trouble of door-to-door delivery."

"Sounds good to me, man," the guy replied, handing over the larger of the two pizzas as the elevator stopped at the fourth floor. "Have a good night."

"You too," I said, stepping out and heading down the hallway to Lia's apartment.

Knocking on the door, I waited a few moments for Lia to pull it open, only to be both surprised and relieved to see her in a pair of sweatpants, her hair up in a bun, and her glasses perched on her nose. To me, that meant she didn't see tonight as a Valentine's Day date, and I was grateful.

"Hey," I said, shrugging off my jacket as I handed over the pizza. "I hope you don't mind, I intercepted the pizza guy on the way up."

"You didn't have to do that," she replied, a warm kindness shining in her eyes, "but thank you."

"No problem."

"So," she started, closing the door and leading me into the living room, "I've got Netflix pulled up on the TV and I promise, this apartment—" Putting the pizza down on the coffee table, she spread her arms out wide, gesturing to the space around us, "—is a completely hockey free zone tonight."

An appreciative smile pulled at my lips. "Thanks," I said as I walked around the back of the couch, my eyes scanning the room. I hadn't been to her apartment other than to pick her up, and other than a few cute trinkets filling the open space, the thing I was most surprised to see was her desk. Which, besides the two screens and the keyboard, was covered entirely with pens, papers, and small sticky notes—all of which I assumed contained information pertaining to her defense. Nodding over to the mess as I took a seat, I asked, "Did you get much work done today?"

Because even though it was a weekend, I knew how determined she was to formulate the best findings she could for her presentation.

"A bit, yeah," she admitted, "though I should tell you to pretend that part of the apartment isn't here. It's a bit of a minefield to most people."

I shrugged. "I think it shows that you're serious about your work, and clearly passionate enough to jot down any idea that could help you get to where you need to be."

"Interesting way of looking at it." Her lips curved into a smile as she popped open the pizza box and motioned for me to grab a slice. Picking up the remote, she said, "Tell me to stop when you see something you like."

If I was in higher spirits, I might've turned to her and made a suggestive comment—alluding to liking her quite a bit—but I stayed quiet. Taking a bite out of my slice, I sat back, my eyes scanning the screen, yet barely registering the movies.

Until The Mighty Ducks popped up on the end of a row of family film recommendations.

"That was the first hockey movie my parents ever showed me," I said, unable to stop the admission as it came spilling out.

Lia's hand froze on the remote as she glanced back and forth between me and the screen a couple of times, a quizzical look on her face. "Mighty Ducks?"

I nodded, casting my eyes down to my lap. "Yeah. They put me in a playground league when I was four, and since I was small for my age, I couldn't really hold my balance all that well. And though I don't remember it, my parents love telling others about how I supposedly wanted to quit at the end of that first year, since I wasn't all that good. Until they showed me The Mighty Ducks, and then I apparently stopped at nothing to be the best in my hometown."

Peeking over her way when she stayed silent, I saw her expression soften as she tucked her legs up underneath her and turned to face me. Her gaze strong yet understanding as she reached out a hand to rest on my knee. "Derrick, did you want to talk about it?" she asked softly. "I know I might not be the best person to talk things through with, but I can be a soundboard if you want to vent. I can listen."

"I know. I know," I said, running a hand through my hair before dropping my head to rest against the back of the couch. "And I'm sorry I kind of shut down the last time you tried. I just don't think I'd really come to terms with it yet. I mean, I still haven't." I sighed. "How can I when my life could be uprooted completely in less than ten days? And I can't do anything. All I can do is wait, staring the trade deadline in the face, and wait for the front office to make a decision."

"Do you have any idea where you might end up?"

"According to my agent, Jersey, Nashville, and L.A. are interested."

"Well, L.A. wouldn't be horrible, right?" she asked, her hand slowly massaging my thigh. Though it wasn't at all suggestive — it was supportive. "You'd be closer to your family at least. And sometimes good opportunities come in roughed up packages."

A single huff of a laugh left my lips as they curved upward slightly, and ever so slowly, I could feel the tension in my shoulders begin to melt away under her soft gaze.

"So... Mighty Ducks?" she asked, nodding back to the television.

Looking back at the screen, I shook my head. "No, not tonight." She'd been right. Tonight wasn't about hockey. Reaching my arm over to wrap around her shoulders, I pulled into my side. "Let's go with Lord of The Rings."

She turned her face up towards mine, her mouth kicking up at one corner. "Really?"

I kissed her quickly before nodding. Sometimes you just needed to invest a few hours into your nerdy side. "Start 'er up. And let's demolish that pizza."

Chapter 13

The trade deadline approached faster than I anticipated, and suddenly, it was the last Monday of February and I had a packed day at work, unable to really follow any news around the decisions being made. Though I made sure to message Derrick when I was finally able to find a half hour to take my lunch.

How are you holding up today?

Honestly, I'm on edge. Coach pulled me aside to let me know that the front office definitely has my name in the mix, but I'm still expected to follow today's workflow until anything official comes through.

I'm sorry. I hope things end up going your way, but if they don't, I hope it gets you one step closer to hoisting the Stanley Cup.

No response came through after that, and with the craziness he was likely dealing with, I didn't necessarily expect one to. However, just as I finished my lunch and stepped out of the café I'd popped into, my phone buzzed.

Though it wasn't Derrick. It was my mom.

"Mom? Everything okay?"

Her familiar laughter sounded through the speaker. "Of course, dear. What? A mother can't call and check in on her own daughter?"

"You can," I said, turning my face away from the wind, "but you normally don't during lunch. Or on Mondays."

Normally our weekly catch up took place on Sundays, whenever both my parents and I could find time to talk, though yesterday, while I hadn't been busy, neither of my parents had been free.

"Well, our weekends might be a bit busier out here for the foreseeable future, so these spontaneous calls may become a regular thing."

"Busier?" I chewed my lip with worry, trying to rack my head for something I'd missed over the holidays. Some hint that things may be off, or changing, but I couldn't think of anything. "What do you mean? Should I be worried about something?"

"No, no, really, nothing's wrong. Quite the opposite actually," she responded. "Have you ever heard of San Fran's Food Fantasy?"

"I…think so," I said, trailing off as I remembered where I'd heard that name. "They're a food blog, right?"

"Yeah, they are. And they actually did a piece on the restaurant last week."

"Mom, that's great!"

The joy seeped into her words as she said, "I know, I know. It's crazy, and since the post went live on Wednesday, we've been swamped."

"Well, you've always been popular in the city, so it's about time the rest of the state—and the rest of the country—knows it."

"Thanks, honey." After a short pause, she decided to turn the conversation back around to me. "But what's new with you? I know you've been swamped lately working on your defense."

"It's definitely been busy," I replied as I finally reached my building, stomping the snow off my boots. "Things are going good though. I'm still hoping to make some sort of connection between my research and the rest of the team's, you know, to really solidify that I'm valuable enough to keep around after April, but otherwise, there hasn't been many hiccups."

"You're the most valuable woman I know, Lia, and I'm sure—whether you can strengthen your defense or not—the department will see that."

I sighed, leaning my head against the lobby wall. "I hope so."

"But outside of work, how are you doing? I don't mean to pry, but I know last Sunday you said you had plans that night, and it didn't escape me that it was Valentine's Day, so... is there someone I should know about?" I felt my face heat as I chewed on the inside of my cheek, debating whether to tell her about Derrick, but my lengthy pause was enough of an answer for her. "There is!"

Laughing at her excitement, I said, "Mom, it's nothing serious. I've been out with this guy a few times, but I don't know if it'll last all that much longer."

As in... I didn't think it'd last past today if the Knights shipped him off.

"Well, as long as you're being safe and enjoying yourself, I guess that's all I can ask for."

"I am, mom, don't worry," I mused, because while our lines of communication were pretty open, there were just some things you didn't need to delve into when talking to your mom about your sex life. "But I should go. My lunch break is over and the data from my lab yesterday isn't going to organize itself."

"Okay then. I love you, and don't work too hard."

"I won't," I said, smiling. "And I love you too."

The rest of the day flew by in a blur. After lunch I'd plopped myself down in front of my computer and sorted through all my research for any final points I wanted and needed to address in my defense. I'd experimented with a lot of different techniques—some successful and some not—to transplant specialized proteins I'd manufactured into living cells, and while I knew I'd done great work here, I also felt like I was only at the cusp of discovering something more. Something more than I could've imagined when I'd started years ago.

But nothing was jumping out to me. Not in my data, not in my handwritten notes, and not in my very rough draft of a report. And it was incredibly frustrating.

As it approached five, I felt a headache begin to thrum behind my eyes and knew I needed to wind down for the day. Rubbing the bridge of my nose as I closed my eyes for a moment, I was spooked when the door opened suddenly.

"Rough day?" Miles asked as he walked into our office, and I spun around in my chair to face him. Coat on and bag over his shoulder, he'd clearly only come by to grab something before leaving for the day, and when he reached for two books that'd been stacked on the far side of his desk, my theory was proved correct.

"No," I said, sighing, "just long."

He chuckled. "I totally feel you on that one. Though hopefully these kinds of days will be behind us soon."

"Here's hoping."

"Speaking of which," he said, sitting on the edge of his desk, "do you happen to have a bit of time over the next day or so to look through my report? As a second set of eyes, you know, to poke holes, ask questions, point out where things aren't flowing properly, or my conclusions don't seem strong enough."

Though I could've declined, busy with my own work, I knew his defense was set a few weeks earlier than my own, and I didn't want to leave him hanging. Plus, I was very likely going to need his same expertise when it came to reviewing my report.

"Yeah, I should," I replied. "If you send over the file, I can take a look tonight and leave my comments."

"Thanks, Lia," he said, looking down at his phone as he pulled up the file on there and shared it. "There, all sent."

Turning back around to my screen, I moved the mouse over to my email tab and sure enough, there was a new message giving me access to his report. "Got it."

"Great, thanks again, and I promise I'll repay the favor when you need it."

My lips curved slightly as I looked back over my shoulder and saw him leaving. "Noted."

And while I very well could've begun packing up to head home myself, I figured I might as well take a peek at his report to see how much work I was in for tonight.

And if it could be done with wine.

Opening the file, my eyes widened when I saw the report was a whopping eighty-three pages, though as I scrolled quickly to the bottom, luckily, more than half of those made up the appendices. Forty wasn't horrible, especially because I saw more than enough graphs and tables taking up a sizeable amount of space.

Going back to the top, I took a quick look at his results section, intrigued by the way he'd laid out his research. In no way was I looking at them with the critical eye that was needed, that is, until

I briefly glanced over the graphs for one of his spotlighted findings. Findings I'd reviewed with him before. Though seeing the results in this new form immediately had the gears in my mind turning.

The way two of his successful experiments for creating cellular metabolism began using cells with very similar characteristics to a pair of cells I'd created artificially.

Clicking back over to my own research to confirm my suspicions, a new hypothesis began to form. With my brain working overtime, I barely had a spare second to think about my actions as I leaped out of my chair and made my way to Professor Klein's office, hoping she hadn't already left for the day.

Luckily, she was seated behind her desk and as I skidded to a stop in her office doorway, she lifted her head with a quizzical expression. "Lia, anything I can help you with?"

"Yes. No. I don't know," I said in a rambling fashion before taking a moment to breathe. "Well, the thing is, I was just reading through Miles' draft report and one of his experiments caught my eye." As I talked through the rest of my ideas—explaining the brief results I'd seen in Miles' work, how they could possibly link up to my own research, and my preliminary suggestions about how the processes could be modified to fuse together—I paced the length of her office. Step after step, my words continued to flow, and when my spew of thoughts came to an end, I turned to Professor Klein and waited for a response.

"That...could be a big discovery, Lia," she said, clasping her hands together atop her desk. "If you're correct, that could be a huge step forward for this department. How sure are you on this?"

"I can't say for certain yet, but my guess would be 75-80%. If I can reproduce the same type of cells using some of the top methods

I've researched, and then link those cells to the beginning of his metabolic tests in the lab with satisfactory results, I believe we'll be able to build more comprehensive strategies off those results and move closer toward fully functioning synthetic cells."

"Then I'll recommend to the department that your defense be moved back until the end of April," she said. Picking up a pen, she wrote down a quick set of notes on the notepad in front of her before meeting my gaze again. "You'll have an extra five weeks to prepare some preliminary findings for this theory of yours, and if you can get lab results to prove it, well, let's just say the chances the department decides to keep you on and offer you the lecturing position increase monumentally."

"Understood."

This was it. The chance I needed to prove to both myself and the department that I was the right fit to stick around and continue my work with the university. It certainly wouldn't be easy, and would likely mean countless late nights over the next month and extra work on the weekends to get these experiments done on time, but I'd do it.

I had to do it.

As a woman in STEM, even with the strides made over the last decade, there were only a limited amount of opportunities available. So when one came along, there was no other choice but to grab it and hold on with all your might.

When I arrived home, there was a sense of excitement in my chest. A giddiness at what tomorrow would bring, but all it took was one phone call from Esme to turn my mood on its head.

"Did you see?" she'd asked, almost nervously.

"See what?"

"The hockey headlines."

And then it hit me like a ton of bricks. The trade deadline.

My research and new ideas had completely consumed my afternoon. So much so that I hadn't glanced at my phone since hanging up with my mom, and sure enough, as I clicked out of the call and opened up Twitter, I saw Boston's number one trending topic was about the Knights.

More specifically, about Derrick.

And as I sank down on the couch, phone in hand, I felt a rough grip squeeze tightly around my heart as my eyes scanned the headline.

DERRICK WELLSLEY HEADS TO LOS ANGELES. NEW ROAD AHEAD FOR THE KNIGHTS.

Chapter 14

It hadn't been a shock that the Knights had moved forward with their plan to trade me, not really, but the way it'd ended up going down—man, was it rough.

The hours had been winding down to the deadline, yet through morning workout, practice, and the team meeting after, not a word came down from the front office. In fact, for a few moments, there'd been a growing bubble of hope that the stress I'd been shouldering the last couple weeks would simply fall away. That there'd be no trade, and nothing would change.

Boy was I wrong.

When the team returned to the locker room after watching game film, the team's general manager was waiting. Waiting for me. Waiting to rip me from my teammates, and without the decency to pull me aside, he began his address in front of them.

"Wellsley," he'd said with a strong and commanding tone, "you'll need to collect your things and say your goodbyes. The Royals are expecting you at their practice facility tomorrow morning, and you've got a spot booked on a flight out in four hours." There was no wavering from his side, even as I stood stock still, absorbing his words despite the uncomfortable gazes coming from the guys around me. "Your agent has been notified and sent the appropriate information, and we advise you speak with him before meeting with your new team in Los Angeles. And finally, thank you." He offered his hand, and not fully processing, I shook it. "Thank you for the work you've put into this team the last couple of years. We appreciate it and can't wait to see your career grow with your new team."

It was to the point, informational, and absolutely heartless.

The next hour was a haze of goodbyes, see-you-soons, and the most awkward ride back to the apartment with Nyberg. Though now it was only his apartment, and his alone.

"This isn't how I wanted today to go, you know," he said, brows furrowed as he leaned against the doorway to my room as I pulled together what I could into a suitcase.

"But we both saw it coming," I replied, my voice still void of any emotion. It'd been that way since I'd received the trade news, and honestly, would probably be like that until I got a moment to myself to process that this was really happening.

I was headed back to the west coast. To Los Angeles. To play for the Royals.

Nyberg shrugged. "Doesn't mean it doesn't suck. I mean, who's going to yell at the TV with me while I watch our opponents play one another, or carpool to practice with me, or help out with Scout by taking him on walks?"

Whether it was hearing his name, or the word 'walk', Scout began bounding down the hall, barking up a storm as he skidded into the room. Circling Nyberg for a few seconds, his attention was quickly refocused when he noticed the state of my room. Sniffing around, it was like he could tell that I was packing to leave—and not just for a road trip.

"Hey buddy," I said, combing my hands through his fur as he looked at me with sad dog eyes. "I know you can probably see that I'm leaving, but I just want you to know that it's not by choice. I'd stay with you forever if I could." His tongue darted out to lick my cheek affectionately. "I love you too, but I'm going to need you to pretend Nyberg's your favorite from now on. I know it'll be difficult, but—"

"You do know he's my dog, right?" Nyberg cut in, quirking a brow. "He's always loved me more."

"Are you sure about that?"

"Of course," he said with a scoff, crouching down and tapping his knees. "Scout, come over here boy. Here, Scout."

While my expression didn't show it, it was much to my amusement that Scout glanced his way for a moment before nuzzling his nose into my neck.

"See," I said, wrapping both arms around Scout as I hugged him close, "he loves me more."

"He's only being affectionate because he can sense you're leaving," Nyberg grumbled, though his features became sheepish as he realized what he'd said. "Not that, you know, you leaving is a good thing or anything, just—"

"Don't worry, I got what you meant."

Apparently this trade was also affecting the way one of my best mates shot the shit with me off the ice. Great.

"Speaking of which," I said, running my hand through my hair as I stood up, "think you can drop me off at the airport? I should be done with this mess in twenty minutes or so."

"Sure thing man, whatever you need."

"And about rent..."

"Don't even worry about it, man."

"But—"

"Seriously dude, don't worry about it," he said adamantly. "I know we leased this place together and you feel responsible for your half, but I'm more than capable of paying the full rent. I mean, you know my salary, it's not going to put that much of a dent in my finances. Maybe I'll even turn your room into a workout space." His lips curved during his attempt at a joke, but the expression swiftly turned sober as his gaze arced around the room. "All you need to be worried about moving forward is how you're going to fit into the Royals lineup and what the next couple months in L.A. are going to look like. No need to be thinking about Boston."

His words made a small fracture in the armor that I'd built after receiving the trade news, making it evident that I was leaving a lot more than just a team here. I was leaving men that had become my brothers over the years, and Nyberg was the closest of them all. Now, instead of being a few meters away, he'd be miles away. A country would span between us, and while I knew we'd stay in touch, it really was the end of an era for our friendship.

"Thanks, man," I said, clearing my throat in an effort not to get choked up. Walking over, I pulled him into a tight embrace and clapped him on the back. "I'm going to miss you."

Though Nyberg's voice seemed just as scratchy as mine as he returned the hug and said, "I'm going to miss you too."

"Well, I guess this is it then," Nyberg said as he pulled into a drop-off parking space at Logan Airport. "At least until you're out here with the Royals in a few weeks for a game."

Because as if starting with another team mid-season wasn't stressful enough, this season's schedule had me flying back out to Boston to play the Knights in just three weeks' time.

"I guess it is," I replied. Not wanting to get into another goodbye like back at the apartment, I unbuckled and grabbed my carry-on from the back seat. "Thanks for the ride, and I'll call you once I'm settled to coordinate shipping my truck and the rest of my shit out."

"Sounds good." He hooked a thumb over his shoulder. "You need help with the stuff in the trunk?"

I shook my head. "I'm good." Holding my fist out, he bumped his own against mine. "I'll see you later."

"Later."

It took a while to locate a luggage cart to load my bags on, because while I'd only had about forty minutes to pack up all I could, I also had my hockey equipment and game day suits to lug across the country. Which left me with three large bags and a backpack as I waved once more to Nyberg and stepped through the automatic doors of Logan International.

Though I was thoroughly unprepared for what awaited me.

Before I could make it to the Delta baggage drop and check-in, a small huddle of photographers and sports journalists spotted me and immediately jumped at their chance for a story.

Having not wanted to deal with the aftermath of the trade becoming official, I'd shot off a quick text to my agent after receiving the news to let him know that I'd call him tonight once I landed before powering down my phone. Though clearly I'd been naïve enough to think that just because I was still letting it sink in, the rest of Boston—hell, the country—would too.

The trade deadline itself was probably one of the top trending things on Twitter right now, and given the speculation around my own situation before things had gone through, I wouldn't be surprised if half the Knights fans in the city were currently letting their thoughts be known right this minute.

And I'd unknowingly walked right into a trap, because of course the press would follow the guy getting booted from his team to the airport.

"Derrick, how does it feel to be leaving Boston after calling it home for more than five years?"

"Did you know Los Angeles was on the table?"

"Are you up for the challenge of navigating a new system of play with the Royals?"

"Do you know how the Royals plan to slot you into their lineup, or are you going in blind?"

"What's going through your head right now?"

The honest answer to that last one was I wanted to be left the fuck alone, but I held my tongue. Trying to maneuver around the small crowd of people was no use, but thankfully as the scene began to draw the attention of others, two guards came over to break things up. It wasn't inconspicuous by any means, but they escorted me to the check-in counter and made sure I passed through security without any press following me.

Meaning I finally had a chance to breathe as I headed for my gate.

Stopping for a quick perusal of snacks, I bought a Gatorade and bag of chips before finding an empty spot in the waiting area, shrugging off my jacket as I took a seat. A jacket that happened to have the Knights' logo and my number on it. Something I definitely wouldn't be wearing again.

Though my hat also had the Knights' logo on it, and while I could've pulled it off as well, I didn't want to risk it being even easier for the people around to recognize me. Instead, I hunched over, cracked open the snacks, and bit the bullet by turning my phone back on—needing something more than just my own thoughts to pass the time until my flight boarded.

Sure enough, once things were powered up, a myriad of notifications began to blow up my screen. Messages from friends, family, and Knights players saying they'd keep in touch. Coach Davidson letting me know he wanted to hop on a call once I'd settled in Los Angeles. Missed calls and numerous voicemails. Facebook and Twitter notifications from strangers and friends alike tagging me in posts about the trade news. It was an overload—exactly what I didn't need.

Wanting to simply play Candy Crush in peace, I pulled up the settings to turn airplane mode on and put a stop to it all, but before I could, a call came through.

A call from Lia.

While my thumb had been hovering over the decline button, something inside me drew me towards accepting the call.

"Hello."

"Derrick, hi," she said with a squeak, seemingly surprised that I'd picked up. "Sorry, I was so busy at work this afternoon that I just saw the news and didn't know if you would pick up. If you were ignoring everyone or already on your way to Los Angeles or what."

Somehow, her rambling was able to sprout the smallest of smiles on my lips. "Well, hopefully you had a better day at work than I did," I said, trailing off as I picked at a loose thread on my sweatpants.

"I... did," she replied carefully. "But that's not why I'm calling. I don't know if you want to talk about it, and obviously if you don't, that's cool and I totally understand, but I figured you wouldn't have wanted to talk about everything with your teammates. Or former teammates, I guess. So, this is me volunteering to be the person you can bitch to about being traded."

A low chuckle escaped me. "So eloquently put."

"And if not today, I'm just a phone call away."

"No, right now is fine, I guess. I'm just at the airport waiting to head out," I said, fixating my gaze on the window, watching the planes land and take off as I recounted the events that'd led to this moment. It wasn't necessarily fun, rehashing how everything had gone down, but it was therapeutic, being able to actually let my anger come through as I spoke.

"Wow," Lia said once all was said and done. "So they really just up and fired you in front of everyone and then fed you to the wolves with the press?"

When she put it that way—so straightforward and blunt—it hurt even more to think about. "I mean, fired is a bit of a stretch since I technically still have a spot in the league, but yeah, more or less."

"What assholes."

"I knew it was coming though, and I guess I can vaguely re-member a few other players over the years being told they'd been traded in front of the rest of the guys, but I never imagined I'd be in that situation."

"Still... the Knights are going to regret letting you go."

"We'll see."

"They will," she reiterated sharply. "You're going to go out to Los Angeles, gel with the guys on the Royals, and make a great run for the Cup in the playoffs. Hell, soon enough you'll probably look back on your time with the Knights and be thankful they traded you."

"I don't know about that."

"Too much?" she asked sheepishly.

"Maybe a little," I mused, "but thanks for the vote of confidence."

"No problem. You're a great player, Derrick, and just because you'll be playing for another team now, that doesn't change the fact that you have skills. Skills millions wish they could have."

"I know, I think it'll just be a bit of a readjustment once I get out there," I said, pausing for a moment before taking the opportunity to address the other elephant in the room. Or elephant on the line. "Speaking of which..."

"Yeah," she replied softly, trailing off with the understanding of where I was going.

"With me out in Los Angeles, we won't really be able to see each other all that much. I know you're busy with your research and I'm going to be up to my neck in new plays as I figure out how to fit into the team dynamic, so—"

"Derrick, it's fine, really," she insisted, her voice genuine. "We've been casual about things for a reason, and I think we both knew this was coming."

"Right," I said, nodding, "but I guess I was wondering how you felt about still being friends? Because while the sex was obviously great—"

She laughed. "Obviously."

"—so were conversations like this one." It'd been so long since I'd been comfortable talking about anything and everything with someone, because while my teammates had been close, we didn't really chat about things below surface level. And now I was leaving all those guys behind too. I needed one constant to hold onto as I headed out west, and I wanted it to be Lia. "So… what do you say?"

"About being friends?"

"Yeah."

"Derrick, we are friends. Just because the dates and sex are going away, that doesn't change things."

"Great," I chirped, a little too happily. A wave of relief rushed through me, knowing this wasn't a goodbye call, but there was also a part of me that wanted her to know I did want to see her again, if the chance came up. Clearing my throat, I continued. "You know, the Royals are playing the Knights in a few weeks, so I'll be back in Boston for a day or two. If you wanted to catch up that is."

"Yeah, just let me know when you're around and I'll see if I'm free," she replied. "Until then, I'll be drowning in all the extra work I made for myself before my defense."

"You're going to kill your defense, so just have that in the back of your mind when you're working."

"And you're going to kill it with the Royals, Derrick. I'll make sure to tune in to a game or two when I get the chance."

We stayed on the phone for a few minutes more, but before I knew it, an announcement that my flight was boarding sounded over the speakers and I ended the call, hopeful I'd talk to her again soon.

Whenthey called my zone for boarding, I pulled my hat down further—one I reallyneeded to trash at the first opportunity—and joined the line. And once I'dshown my ticket, that was that. Though my chin hung low, my feet moved forward,and I didn't look back as I boarded the plane headed for Los Angeles.

Chapter 15

How was your first night in your new city?

Pretty boring. Headed straight to the hotel the team is putting me up in for the next couple weeks until I find a place to live. But at least they had room service.

So you had a burger and fries before crashing is what you're saying?

How'd you know?

We both know airplane food is shit. Plus, I figured you'd want some comfort food.

You're right on both accounts, but I've got to get going. Meeting with Royals management at eight.

Good luck! And talk to you later.

Well, first day as a Royal wasn't so bad. The guys seem chill and were quick to give me some pointers on how to acclimate to the city. Plus, my new coach is meeting with me 1-on-1 before practice tomorrow to go over the team's power play.

That's great!

Yeah, hopefully it'll be a good fit for me.

Are you just back in your hotel then?

Yup. A few guys brought me out to a local pizza place for dinner, but now I'm just watching Toronto whoop Florida's ass.

I'd believe it.

But hey, what about you? How's this mountain of work you said you had coming along? Find a way for life to survive on Mars yet?

Haha, I wish. But it's... slow going. Basically, I may have found a way to combine two areas of focus in my department to reach the next level of research in the field, but I have to have concrete proof that it's viable to be able to include it in my defense.

Damn, and all I do every day is skate around with a stick and a puck.

You know you do a lot more than that.

I do, but it's definitely not as important. I'm going to leave you to your work while I try to get used to this time zone.

Good luck with that, considering you're traveling to St. Louis in two days.

Thanks for reminding me.

Great game tonight!

Thanks.

Nobody expected you to be perfect your first night in a Royals jersey, but you got things under control and got an assist in the third – I'd call that a win.

So you actually watched?

Told you I would.

Should I lease a condo or find an apartment to rent?

Renting a house a no-go for you then?

Too much space for just me.

Then I'd probably say condo. They're usually nicer... right?

You wanna see the four choices I'm deciding between?

Sure, send them over.

Did you hear about the blizzard that happened here last night?

Considering the Knights' flight back home was delayed after their game in Montreal, I certainly did. Nyberg was bitching about it.

He was right to bitch! It's impossible for me to get to campus today so I'm stuck without my lab results until tomorrow, if the city even gets the snow cleared by then. It's still coming down pretty bad.

So now wouldn't be the best time to talk about how weird it feels to be living in a city where the temperature's above 80 in March?

YOU THINK?

My truck finally got here. No more driving around in this stupid little rental.

A little piece of Boston with you out in California.

How's the research coming along?

You know it's nearly eleven here, right?

Ahh, sorry, I sometimes forget time zones are a thing. I usually just rely on the time on my phone to be correct with all the traveling I do.

No worries – just wanted to point it out. I actually just finished things up for the night and I made some real progress.

Any chance you want to regale me with this progress over the phone. I may be just a bit bored.

I could... but no promises I stay awake long enough to get through it all.

1 MISSED CALL

Sorry, I was in the lab when you called earlier. Was it important?

Nothing urgent. Just wanted to check if you're free to grab lunch on Friday. The team plane lands at midnight the night before, and Coach knows I have to wrap things up with Nyberg and the apartment in the morning, so I'm only expected to be at the arena for pre-game skate at 3.

I'm free on Friday, but any chance we can meet near the university? My car's been on the fritz again lately.

Can do! Anywhere particular you have in mind?

Whatever's good with you is good with me.

I squinted at the screen, lifting my glasses as I leaned in—as if that would magically solve the problem with my spreadsheet that I couldn't seem to find. Some of my results from the tests I'd run over the past three weeks were coming out similar to how I'd hoped, while two runs had damaged the cells to a point that the proteins had become denatured and were unable to perform the function they'd been built to.

The data I was studying tonight, however, had come from the experiment I let sit overnight before recording the results bright and early this morning. There had to be something wrong with my calculations though, because at first glance, the experiment had appeared successful. The proteins looked strong, the cells had held up, and I'd gotten sufficient data showing the cells ability to metabolize under the conditions I'd set. The only problem was the graph that'd come up once I'd pulled the metabolic data over. Instead of its usual shape—spiking early before decreasing over several hours—there was a second spike.

Which just didn't make sense.

Until I realized the problem wasn't with the data, but the spreadsheet itself. For some reason, the formula I had used to calculate the oxygen concentration in the cells hadn't been copied over correctly for ten of the values, causing an anomaly with my graph.

A silly mistake. One of several I'd made lately, though I'd luckily caught them all before they'd affected anything significantly. Whether they were due to the lack of sleep—because who had time to sleep when they had such a tight deadline—or the extra caffeine, however, was anybody's guess.

Though it wasn't outside of the realm of possibility for my attention to be wavering because of the countless hours I spent working—more or less from the moment I woke up every morning until I went to bed. If I ate, I typically ate in front of a screen. If I took a break, I had my phone in my hand to jot down notes or theories that could help with my next round of tests. And even when I tried to wind down and get ready for bed, my mind was always working. The cogs never completely shutting off.

Which, in retrospect, I knew wasn't healthy. After all, the same kind of work ethic had caused a similar, yet much worse, tailspin back when I'd started my PhD. But this was different. I only had two weeks—three at max—to wrap up my testing and results before I had to get to work on the new version of my final report and presentation.

This craziness had a deadline.

One that I was well too aware of.

However, I was snapped out of my internal worry when I heard three raps on my apartment door.

Furrowing my brows as I glanced toward the doorway, I waited a few seconds to see if whoever it was would knock again. And they did.

Confused, because I knew I hadn't buzzed anyone in, I stood up and walked over to the door. Peering into the peephole, I saw Esme and Harper's familiar faces looking back at me. It'd been over two weeks since I'd seen them face to face—the last time being the morning of the trade deadline when we'd met up for our weekly Monday morning catch ups. The last two Mondays, however, I'd skipped, choosing instead to start early in the lab.

In fact, now that I thought about it, I'd skipped out on a lot of things outside of work.

For good reason, in my opinion, but I'd still done it.

Opening the door, I shot them both a look of curiosity. "Hey," I said, waving them in. "What are you guys doing here?"

They eyed one another as I closed the door behind them. "Well, we just wanted to check in on you," Esme said, a carefulness to her words. "We know you've been really busy these last couple weeks, and—" She glanced in the direction of my desk, which was, of course, a tornado of a mess. "—we wanted to make sure you weren't over doing it."

"Yeah, I'm fine," I was quick to respond.

Harper quirked a brow. "You sure?"

"I mean... mostly," I said meekly before sighing and running my fingers through my hair. "It's just, a lot is going on right now with work." I walked over to my couch and sank onto it. "Even though my defense got pushed back to accommodate my latest hypothesis, I'm more or less trying to cram a semester's worth of experiments into a few weeks while still prepping lessons and help sessions for the students I'm teaching."

Moving to sit next to me, Harper wrapped her arms around my shoulders. "But it's all going to pay off in the end."

"And we know your plate is full, don't worry. We're not asking you to abandon your work," Esme said, walking over to my desk and eyeing all the notes. "We know this is important to you and it's crunch time, we just want to make sure you're taking care of yourself."

I sank into Harper's hug and lifted the corners of my mouth. "And I appreciate it."

"So, we thought we'd suggest a break," Harper said. I craned my neck to look at her incredulously, but before I could speak, she continued. "Not a long one. Just an hour or so. Long enough for the three of us to catch up and then we'll get out of your hair for the night."

"Besides, it's eight 'o'clock on a Thursday, Lia, and I bet you haven't taken a break other than to eat since you got up this morning." Esme stared me down. "If you even ate."

"I did. Three times plus snacks," I said with reassurance. "Though I may have worked while I ate."

"See," Harper said. "You need a short break. One where you're not focused on work."

"Fine," I grumbled, giving in.

"Don't sound so excited," Esme chirped sarcastically, causing me to laugh.

"Sorry, you know I didn't mean it like that."

Honestly, I probably did need this break. With the way I'd more or less been avoiding everything in my life outside of work lately, I could use the hour to recharge. To hopefully get my mind in a better place.

And when my cell buzzed moments later, I asked Esme to grab it from my desk as she came to join Harper and I on the couch. Which may have been a mistake, seeing as she not-so-subtly glanced at the screen before handing it over.

"I'm sorry... why is Derrick texting you?"

"Didn't you two split when he left for Los Angeles?" Harper asked, her interest as keen as Esme's as I snatched the phone away.

"Clearly not," Esme mused, "considering he wanted to know if the Italian diner by the university was a good place to meet tomorrow."

Harper's expression filled with amusement. "Oh really?"

"It's not that big of a deal," I said, glancing down at the screen to confirm that the text from Derrick had really said that. And it did, somehow prompting a blush to rise on my cheeks. "He's flying in tonight for the game tomorrow and wanted to meet up for lunch."

"And you said yes?"

"Why wouldn't I? I mean, we were friends with benefits, and just because the benefits are gone, that doesn't mean the two of us have to go back to being strangers."

"So you're saying you guys still talk?" Harper asked.

"We text," I admitted. "And there may have been a phone call here or there."

"Well at least we know that not all your time has gone into your work over the past two weeks," Esme said slyly, nudging my side playfully. "But couldn't you have picked a guy that, I don't know, still lives in the city to be your distraction."

I shook my head. "He's not a distraction. It's not like that. But speaking of guys in the city, did I tell you Miles tried to ask me out to drinks the Friday after the trade deadline? Just the two of us."

Both of their eyes widened. "As a date?"

"Not explicitly, but I figured that's what he meant. It was like he knew Derrick was out of the picture, so he tried to jump at his chance."

"And you said no?"

"Of course I said no. I'm not interested in Miles, and if he was angling for a date, I wasn't about to lead him on."

The two of them stared at me with disbelief, clearly not having prepared for all the things they'd missed with me sinking into deep work mode the last few weeks.

"Wow, you've really left us out of the loop when it comes to your love life drama."

"Trust me, right now, I wish I was out of the loop. All I really want right now is to get through my final round of experiments and get this defense finished."

"But you're still meeting up with Derrick tomorrow?" Harper asked, and I confirmed with a shy nod. "Are you sure that's a good idea?"

Biting the inside of my cheek, I sank back into the couch cushions helplessly. "We'll have to wait and see."

Chapter 16

"You sure your new team is going to be okay with you bringing two extra suitcases back on the flight?" Nyberg asked.

With my knees on top of my second suitcase to weigh it down, I finished zipping it up before glancing back at him. "They're going to have to be."

I had let my Coach know I'd be flying back with my remaining belongings tomorrow morning, though to be fair, I hadn't specified how much. I figured I'd be able to squeeze everything into a large suitcase. Though I'd underestimated. It'd taken a trip to the department store for another suitcase to finish packing my clothes and the rest of my belongings that I'd left lying around the apartment, and even that was a tight squeeze.

"Well, if you do need to lose some weight in those bags, I'll happily take the PS4 off your hands."

"I'm sure you would." I chuckled as I stood up, dusting my hands off on my jeans. "In fact, I'm surprised you didn't try to hide it and keep it for yourself."

"Thought about it," he drawled before shrugging, "but it's yours. I'll buy a new one when I get the chance."

"Great." I punched him lightly in the bicep. "Then I can kick your ass from across the country."

A bark of laughter escaped him and he shook his head with amusement. "You're dreaming if you think that's true."

"We'll just have to wait and see then."

The good-natured ribbing continued—back and forth—as we each took one of the suitcases from my now-empty room and rolled them toward the door. We'd already agreed that they'd stay at the apartment for the rest of the day and I'd pick them up early before having to board the team bus to the airport.

"So, do the Royals need extra practice time this afternoon to get ready to face us?" Nyberg asked teasingly. "Or do you have time to grab lunch?"

"You forget that I know all your moves, so you can bet we'll be ready to put up a fight," I replied before rubbing my chin a few times with my right thumb. "But, uh, I can't do lunch."

He lifted a brow. "Oh?"

"Yeah, I—"

My phone buzzed in my pocket, cutting me off as I pulled it out to see a message from Lia confirming we were still meeting in half an hour. And knowing how tightly packed her schedule was lately at work, I quickly shot off a reply.

"I'm assuming you have other plans?"

"What?" My gaze snapped back up to meet his as I tucked my phone away. "Oh, yeah. I'm, uh, actually meeting up with Lia before I head to practice." While I expected some sort of reaction, it was a bit surprising to see how quickly his expression shifted. Suddenly he was looking at me like I'd been transformed into a unicorn right before his very eyes. "What?"

"Nothing," he replied, shaking himself out of it. "Sorry, I just didn't know the two of you were still talking. I thought, you know, you would've cut her loose by now with the move."

"I mean, I sort of did," I admitted. "But we're friends."

He shot me a look of disbelief. "Friends?"

"Yeah, friends," I confirmed. "And just because I'm not on the east coast because the fucking Knights didn't want to keep me, that doesn't mean I'm just going to toss that away."

Bringing his hands up defensively, he said, "Woah, man, calm down. I didn't mean it like that."

I sighed. "I know you didn't."

"And you know I couldn't have stopped the trade if I tried. That's not how the league works. We all miss you here, but maybe, just maybe, Los Angeles really is what's best for your game right now. I mean, me and some of the guys have been watching your games and you're making a difference."

Lifting the corner of my mouth, I said, "Enough to trample you guys tonight, hopefully."

"Good luck getting a shot passed me," he said, hitting his chest in confidence. "But back to Lia," he continued, scrutinizing my expression for some sort of hidden answers, "you guys kept in touch?"

"Yeah," I conceded, though held up a hand before he could cut in. "But it's nothing serious. It never has been."

"Really?" he asked flatly.

"Really."

"Okay, okay." He nodded, though it was clear he didn't believe me. "Then tell me, how often do you guys talk? A few times a week?" He lifted a brow. "Every day?"

"Uh, I don't know. Most days, I guess."

Usually at night or during our spare moments, when the two of us weren't neck deep in our respective work. Though I kept that to myself.

"And would it be weird if you guys suddenly stopped talking? Not a peep. Just full radio silence?"

I exhaled slowly, combing my fingers through my hair. "I don't know, man. I mean, yeah, it would be."

"So, hear me out for a second," he said. "Maybe you should talk to Lia about the fact that you guys are in a relationship, but you just haven't put a label on it."

I was about to refute his words, except when I went to open my mouth, another voice spoke up in the back of my head.

What if he was right?

Back in Los Angeles there'd been a woman or two who'd chatted me up while out for drinks with my new teammates, but each time, I'd see a text come through from Lia and suddenly any attraction I had to them was shut down. I'd chalked it up to tiredness or me simply not being interested, but what if it was more than that?

What if I did have feelings for Lia?

Shit.

And when Nyberg laughed, I realized I'd said that last part out loud.

"It's not the end of the world, mate."

"I know, I know." I could feel my lips turn downward in a frown. "I'm just not really a relationship person. Not anymore."

He clapped me on the shoulder. "Oh, trust me, I know. But not all relationships end in a dumpster fire."

"And how would you know?"

"I wouldn't, but I can think of a handful of people that can personally attest to it. Guys on the team, my brother, and hell, aren't your parents still together?" They were. "My point is, one bad experience—"

"You mean fucking awful experience?" I muttered.

His mouth curved with amusement. "Sure. But still, one fucking awful experience doesn't mean another relationship can't work out. And the only way to figure out if it can work is to talk about it. Preferably with Lia and not me."

There was no denying that he was right, because there was something about Lia I couldn't shake. Something that had gotten under my skin. But what exactly it was? There was a list.

It could've been the shyness that bloomed into an intelligent, sexy woman. Her love of sports balanced out with an understanding of how hectic my schedule was. Her dedication to her research that mirrored—and exceeded—that of guys I'd seen give everything to be the best in the game. And our chemistry, man was it off the charts. Even after having not seen each other in weeks, I could still feel that heat and want building in my chest. Like a balloon waiting to pop.

And, as scary as it was to admit to myself, I needed to know if Lia felt the same. I needed to know if I had to trample these embers of feelings once and for all or go down the far riskier route of seeing where things with her could lead.

I wasn't completely naïve though. There were obvious variables in the way, but as thoughts of her overflooded my mind, I figured there must be a way we could make the equation work.

Twenty minutes later, I was walking into the Italian diner I'd found on Google Maps, a bell ringing above my head as I scanned the room for Lia.

It was a seat yourself type place with red checkered tablecloths on every table, black and white framed photos of iconic Italian landmarks on the walls, and a whole chalkboard wall to the right listing their entire menu in cursive. Classic with a few unique twists, and fairly popular if the number of guests was anything to go by.

And among them, Lia sat near the back left of the restaurant, smiling up at the waitress as I headed over.

"Hey," I greeted. I wanted to lean over to kiss her hello, but restrained myself.

Lia's eyes gleamed as they met mine, though the waitress cut in before she could talk, so she settled for a wave as I took a seat across from her.

"So, I'm guessing you're the man we're waiting for?" I nodded. "Could I get you something to drink?"

"I'll just take a water, thanks."

Leaving the two of us to peruse the menu, she promised to be back in a few minutes.

"Well, this place is cool," I said, trying to come off calm, cool, and collected despite the nerves eating up my mind. Eventually I'd have to steer this conversation into a more serious one, but in that moment, I was honestly happy just sitting across from her. "Have you ever been here before?"

"Twice. It only opened a year or two ago, but it's been pretty popular among the student crowd since it's fairly cheap," she replied before the fingers on her left hand began to fiddle with the edge of the tablecloth.

"Nervous about something?" I teased, nodding to her hand.

She smiled sheepishly, a blush coating her cheeks at having been caught. "Sorry. It's just, even though it's been less than three weeks, it's a bit weird seeing you again." She lifted a shoulder, biting her lip. "I missed you."

Those three words were exactly what I needed to hear.

My grin widened as I reached across the table to intertwine our fingers. "I missed you too."

Every part of her expression seemed to radiate joy at my response. Her eyes were brighter, her cheeks redder, her grin bigger, and when she squeezed my hand, she didn't let go.

"How are you finding Los Angeles?" she asked, lifting a brow. "I know we've talked since you moved, but how are you really finding living out in California compared to Boston?"

"Well, considering I've been traveling half that time, it hasn't sunk in yet, you know? I can tell you that the traffic's a lot worse out there, but otherwise, things have been good so far. The weather's been great, I can move into my condo next week, the guys on the Royals have all been pretty welcoming, and I don't know—" I shrugged, the corner of my mouth quirking upward. "—it kind of feels like going back home. Or at least it's starting to."

"That's great, Derrick."

"I do miss you though," I added. "And I know I already said it, but—"

"I get it," she replied softly.

As I smiled back, the lead in to where I wanted to take this conversation was interrupted by the return of our waitress, and I pulled my hand back from Lia's. Having not really looked over the menu at all, we both quickly scanned the wall before ordering the house lasagna with a side of fried calamari to share.

And it took a while for my courage to come clean about my feelings to build up again. There were moments—in between the bread, the appetizer, and our main meal—where I could've brought it up, and at times the words were on the tip of my tongue, but each time a small seed of doubt would pop into my mind and stop me.

Though once our empty plates were taken away, I knew I was running out of time. Lia was incredibly busy with her research and had likely taken an extended break just to eat with me. I didn't need to be inconveniencing her further, meaning the clock was ticking.

If this was a hockey game, it would be the last seconds of a tied game. I would have control of the puck, and with one last chance, I would've wound up and took my shot.

Which is exactly what I did.

"So," I started, picking nervously at the edges of the napkin that rested on my lap, "I talked to Nyberg this morning."

"How's he dealing living by himself? Or has he found another roommate?"

"He seems fine with it, honestly. I went over to pack up the rest of my stuff and he never mentioned looking for another roommate," I explained. "Though he might come the off-season, who knows. But that's not actually what I wanted to talk about." A tiny crease formed between her eyebrows as she waited for me to continue, and I thought it was incredibly sexy. Also, adorable. "I mentioned I was meeting up with you for lunch and he, uh, kind of said something that resonated with me, but I don't know if it will with you."

"Okay... what was it?"

"He thought that us—me and you—were basically in a relationship, we just weren't putting a label on things."

The way she froze for a moment told me I'd caught her off guard, but I stayed silent, not wanting to push or explain further until she spoke.

"That's, uh, that's, I mean, okay," she rambled, struggling to form a coherent thought.

"I didn't really agree with him at first," I mentioned. "I told him that we'd agreed this had been casual and we were fine with ending things, but the thing that I realized is... we didn't really end things. We stopped seeing each other, for obvious reasons, but the way we talk and catch each other up on our days? That hasn't changed."

She exhaled slowly, letting my words sink in. "No," she said softly. "It hasn't." Her gaze fell to the table as she continued. "And to be fair, Esme and Harper were wondering the same thing when they showed up at my place yesterday. Asking why the two of us were still talking if you'd shipped off to the other side of the country."

"What did you say?"

"I told them we were still friends," she said, chewing on her bottom lip, "just without the benefits."

"And that's what you want?" I asked, praying to hear the word no. I wanted to kiss her. I wanted her support. I wanted her.

Though I was all too aware that what I wanted didn't matter if she didn't want the same thing.

"I—I don't know, Derrick. I mean, that's what we agreed on, right?"

"It was."

"But now you're saying that's not what you want any more."

I shook my head. "This isn't about me. Don't think about my feelings right now," I said, the words falling from my lips as our gazes stayed locked on one another. "What do you want?"

"I—"

She stopped, holding her tongue while her eyes roamed around my features. Looking for the right answer despite the fact that all she had to do was be honest. But maybe that was the problem. Maybe she hadn't been honest with herself.

Letting out a slow breath, she closed her eyes, looked up at the ceiling, and started again. "I honestly didn't start things up with you expecting it to lead to a relationship," she admitted. "You're a great guy, our chemistry is off the charts, and we have fun together, but I never let myself imagine moving further than that. Not really. Mostly because I never saw anything more as an option."

I nodded, but didn't respond, wanting to hear everything she had to say. It didn't matter that each word stung; I masked my emotions.

"There's so much to think about right now because the most important thing to me over the next couple of months is my PhD. I need to stay focused to craft the perfect defense, get the students I'm teaching prepped for finals, and hopefully show the department at Harvard I'm worthy of the lecturing spot I applied for next term."

"And I totally get that."

I couldn't tell if she'd even registered the words that left my mouth—almost involuntarily—as they'd been so quiet. And by the speed in which her rambling continued, my best guess was she hadn't.

"But if I really think about it, I agree with Ryan." My brows shot up at her shy admission and a small amount of hope surged through me. "I like talking to you and catching up on how things are going in your life. I like that even though it was our chemistry that drew us together, our personalities also seem to mesh. I like being there for you and knowing that you're there for me. And I guess I've always thought relationships with a friendship at the foundation were the best kind, but because of how everything started, never let myself think about any feelings that were underneath the surface. But they are. There are feelings there."

It was everything I wanted to hear, yet I didn't realize that I was taking a moment to let it all sink in until Lia began fidgeting.

"Uh, I don't know if you have something to say now, or...?"

"Yeah, right, sorry." I ran a hand through my hair. "As you can probably tell I'm not good at this stuff, and if I'm being honest, the only other relationship I've ever been in ended in a colossal dumpster fire."

"What happened? If you don't mind me asking."

"No, it's fine," I said, knowing it was important to lay everything out on the table. "I got together with my ex, Chelsea, at the end of high school. About a year before I got drafted. And things were great, so we didn't even think about splitting up and stayed together through my early years in the league when I was playing in the minors. The traveling was a lot on her though, but I didn't know that. She was in college, seeing roommates and friends circle through relationships, and didn't fully trust me while I was out on the road.

"On my side though, I had blinders on. I thought I was in love with this great woman who supported my career, who wanted to build a life with me, and someone that ultimately checked off all the boxes for me. I only found out things weren't so great when I popped the question during the off-season when we were both twenty."

The surprise was evident on Lia's face. "You proposed?"

"I did," I confirmed. "And do you want to know what she said?" After a hesitant nod, a humorless laugh escaped me. "She said that I was living a fantasy out on the road and didn't have a grasp on our relationship at all. Apparently, she'd been seeing someone else for over six months because we'd gone that long without seeing each other—the longest over the course of our relationship—and she just wanted to wait to break up in person. She said she couldn't love someone that wasn't there for her both emotionally and physically."

"I'm sorry, but she was completely in the wrong," Lia said, immediately jumping at the chance to make me feel better. "Cheating is the worst thing to do to a person, and if she was having doubts, she should have come to you. Even over the phone."

"I know that now," I replied, "but it took a few years to work through the tainted feelings I had around relationships. Though the constant traveling has always been something that's held me back."

"Why now then?" she asked, her voice timid and curious. "What's changed to make you want a relationship with me of all people? Especially when we're living on opposite sides of the country."

I was all too aware we were still seated in the middle of a restaurant, but this was my one chance to prove my case to her that I was worth it. That this wasn't just the impulsive decision it seemed to be. So, standing up, I watched Lia's eyes widened as I walked around the table and crouched down in front of her. Cupping her chin, I leaned in for a kiss, a smile forming when she didn't pull back.

As our lips met for the first time in three weeks, a rush of desire flowed through me. One that'd been locked behind a gate for far too long and couldn't be extinguished. And from the way Lia gasped before sinking into the kiss, I wanted to believe she was feeling the same.

It was a kiss that I wished I'd kept away from prying eyes—wanting to run my hands all over her body and feel her shiver when I deepened things. But being in public had me holding back; keeping things soft and sweet but still full of passion until I pulled back.

"Because of that," I said, my breath fanning her lips. "Because you're smart, driven, caring, and insanely fucking attractive." She chuckled lightly, smiling as a blush began to tint her cheeks. "Because what's between us could be as electric as lightning if we explored it, and because in just a short amount of time, I feel like we've built up something strong. Something worth fighting for."

Biting her lip, she asked, "Even though you know how I feel about relationships coming before my work?"

"Of course. Hell, my career isn't exactly easy to deal with either," I countered. "I at least know that you're busy trying to change the world, which I could never fault you for. Meanwhile, I'm stuck working on the other side of the country."

"Technically, you work all over the country," she drawled. "Including here."

"On rare occasions, yes. But I need you to be honest with me about this, because you deserve better than a guy hopping around states—"

She leaned in to peck my lips, effectively shutting me up. "I can decide what I deserve."

"And?" I pulled back far enough to meet her eyes. "What's the consensus?"

Her lips curved upward. "That this—" Her hand found mine and squeezed. "—is something I want to explore. And everything else, we can figure out. Together."

Chapter 17

W ith the game about to start, I was shaking the last-minute nerves out alongside my teammates in the tunnel. But for the first time in this arena, it was as a member of the visiting team. I wasn't wearing navy and silver in Boston; I was wearing white and gold.

"How are you feeling?" asked Ruderman, the captain of the Royals, as he sidled up next to me. "Nervous to be back?"

I chuckled. "That obvious?"

"Just a hunch," he mused, nudging my side. "But try not to think about it too much. Most players in the league have to go through this at some point in their career, it's just the nature of the game, so use it as an opportunity. Don't view it as returning to a place that you failed, but rather an organization that failed you. Your old teammates will still be your friends after tonight, so take this moment and show the Knights' management that they made a mistake letting you go. Step out onto the ice and make them regret their decision. Show them who you are and help us slap these guys into next Tuesday."

The corners of my mouth pulled upward, because that was exactly what I needed to hear to stoke the flames burning within me. "Were you also voted team motivational speaker when they made you captain?"

He let loose a bark of laughter. "Comes with the role, my friend." As the announcer's voice rang loud, hyping up the crowd, and when the rest of the guys began heading out to the rink, Ruderman nudged me forward. "Go on. Show everyone what you can do."

Shaking out the last of my nerves, I started down the tunnel amongst my new teammates. The music blasting through the arena's speakers was loud—successfully pumping up the crowd—though it didn't completely drown out the chorus of boos several Knights fans let loose as we skated around our end of the ice.

Which was to be expected. After all, they didn't want us coming in here and handing their team a loss. But that was the plan, so I let the noise fade away, focusing in on the game that was about to start.

Skating twice around our half of the rink, I then joined most of the guys on our bench, leaving the starters out on the ice as we waited for the national anthem to start.

But before it did, my line mate, Quinn, nudged me in the side.

I turned to him and lifted a brow. "What?"

He lifted his stick and pointed to the jumbotron, and when I lifted my gaze in that direction, I was floored by what I saw.

An image of me.

And then another.

And another.

Letting the surrounding noise begin to sink back in, I realized that not only was the announcer mentioning my return to Boston, but the crowd was beginning to cheer for me. And not just with their words. I caught a glimpse of a handful of signs in the stands wishing me well and stating how much they missed me.

"And to welcome him back in style—" I heard the announcer say, bringing my gaze back to the jumbotron. "—let's take a look back at Wellsley's journey with the Knights over the past five years."

The images transitioned into clips from past seasons; from my first game to my first goal as a Knight, from overtime winners to playoff games, and even clips from practices and charity nights where it was clear the bond between me and the guys had been genuine.

It was something that easily could have gotten me choked up in a different setting, but keeping my game face on, the only reaction I gave was a smile, my lips curving upward as the crowd began chanting my name.

Something truly surreal and unexpected, and it meant so much.

As the montage came to an end, fading to black after a clip from the game against Tampa just weeks ago, the announcer said, "And I think I speak for every Knights fan in Boston right now when I say welcome home Wellsley."

The chanting turned to cheering, into hoots and hollers, and even my new teammates joined in, succeeding in cracking my façade even further as they banged their sticks against the boards and clapped me on the shoulder in recognition.

"No easing up on these guys just because they made you a tribute, you hear me?" Quinn said teasingly as the noise began to wind down.

I chuckled, standing as the anthem singer made her way out onto the ice. "You won't see anything less than one hundred percent from me, man."

"Good, because this game is ours."

It was. However, it was also ours to lose.

Once the anthem finished and the guys out on the ice lined up, my walls came back up. Nobody in the stands mattered at this moment. All that mattered was the action out on the rink.

When the puck dropped and the Knights got first possession, we were immediately put on the defensive, but that didn't stop the guys from making moves. The puck went back and forth between teams before finally the Knights took a shot and our goalie covered it clean, prompting the lines to change and giving me my first taste of how it felt to play in this arena on the visitor's side.

"Your team ready to get your ass whooped, Wellsley?" Brookes taunted lightly as the two of us came together for the puck drop. With me gone, he'd stepped up his game and had shown himself to be a power center.

But tonight, he was going down.

"Not a chance."

The Royals won.

Going into the last five minutes of play tied two goals a piece, both teams had zeroed in and were fighting tooth and nail for the game winner. It was scrappy, yet strategic, and being familiar with the Knights' style of play paid off for me. Big time.

With less than a minute left, the Knights were in our zone, passing the puck between them, trying to spot an opening but unable to find one. And all it took was one jump out of position from me, tipping the puck off course with my stick when Orlov shot the puck over to Brookes to start a 2-on-2 race back to the other end of the ice.

My stick handling had been second nature, and having done so in practice for years, I easily deked out the defense and wound up to shoot on Nyberg. Only I didn't, because that was what he was expecting. Instead, I chipped it over to Quinn, who shot a beauty of a one-timer at the top left corner of the net, dinging off the crossbar and down into the net.

And the Knights didn't have time to answer.

When the clock finally hit zero and the buzzer sounded, I stood up from the bench and hopped over the boards with the rest of my teammates as the Knights quickly vacated the ice. However, as I made a move towards our goalie, my teammates chose instead to surround me in a large group hug.

"We did it, boys!"

"Congrats, Wellsley!"

"This one was for you."

It was heartwarming, knowing that these men whom I still didn't know all that well had played today for me. Because most of them knew what it felt like to be in the same situation, and they wanted to give me something to lift my mood. Something to hold on to and something to prove I hadn't been a weak link, but a core part of the Knights' line-up.

Something to carry forward as a Royal—to know that I was the type of player who could make a difference.

The celebration of our win continued into the locker room; the energy of the room high as Coach Lennox walked into the room with a grin on his face.

"Way to fight for the win tonight," he said, clapping to further the enthusiasm. "You guys capitalized on the opportunities you were given and defended well when we had a man in the box. All things that will help us lock down a spot in the playoffs sooner rather than later."

"You know it, Coach!"

He chuckled at Ruderman. "Get yourself dressed, because you're out in front of the press tonight." Which made sense, since he'd picked up a goal and an assist tonight. "And Quinn, you're up too."

"You got it."

Coach nodded. "Now, I know you're all tired, but the last one on the bus is getting an extra round of suicides at tomorrow night's practice."

A round of grumbles and laughs filled the room as Coach turned to leave, and while most of the guys continued stripping off their equipment, I followed him. Not caring that all I'd taken off so far were my helmet and gloves.

"Hey, Coach, wait up," I said, hopping not-so-gracefully over the discarded equipment of the guys around me. "I—"

"Wellsley," he cut me off, sighing as he stopped and turned to face me, "I know you were probably looking to go out there and talk to the press to let them know you'd found your feet with this organization, but I thought it was best to keep the focus on our win. I didn't want everything to suddenly fall on your shoulders, but you did play well tonight. That's not up for debate."

Unexpected, especially since it was actually a relief that I didn't have to go out in front of the reporters. I still hadn't fully recovered from the last shit show, but the encouragement was certainly nice to hear.

"That... actually wasn't what I wanted to talk about."

"Oh." He straightened, a small crease forming on his forehead. "Then what is it?"

"Well, I know you're not exactly policing our rooms tonight or anything—"

"No, sir. Y'all don't need babysitters."

My lips twitched. "Yeah, but I just wanted to let you know that I'm going to be meeting up with some of the Knights for a drink later, and then I'll likely head over to my—" The next word, foreign to me, got stuck on my tongue for a moment. "—girlfriend's for the night."

His brows rose. "Nobody mentioned you left a girlfriend out here, Wellsley."

"Yeah," I chuckled, bringing my hand up to rub the back of my neck. "That's because I technically didn't. We agreed we wouldn't do long distance, but, you know, things changed."

And they changed quickly, apparently. I'd come back to Boston excited to see my friends, play some hockey, and catch up with Lia, and now I was leaving tomorrow with not only a win for the Royals, but a girlfriend.

"Well, I'm not standing in the way of anything," he replied. "I know you've got a life here, and you're off the clock until tomorrow morning. Have fun, just be in the lobby and ready to leave for the airport tomorrow at eight."

"I will be," I agreed before turning to head back to the locker room.

Now that the game was behind me, I was itching to get out of this gear and catch up with the guys, knowing it would be my last time in Boston for a while. And because of that, it felt like time was simultaneously running too fast and too slow as the team packed up and headed out—Lopez, a second-string defenseman, being the unlucky soul who was gifted an extra round of suicides. When we finally got back to the hotel, it was already after nine, and after a quick shower and a change of clothes, I called an Uber to meet up with everyone at Apollo's.

I was expecting a few guys to be there—Nyberg, Brookes, Orlov, maybe Schmidt—but when I walked in closer to ten, after two texts from Nyberg making sure I was still showing up, I was surprised to see almost the entire team had made it out.

"Wellsley," Orlov exclaimed when he saw me, grinning as he raised his beer in greeting. "You came!"

I smiled back, realizing most conversations had died down amongst the group and all eyes were on me. "Of course I came," I said, sidling up to Brookes and nudging his side. "Did you guys think I was going to bail after absolutely annihilating you guys on the ice?"

"Oh, the guy has jokes," Nyberg drawled.

"That he does." I smirked, nodding down to his nearly empty beer. "Did you want another drink? It could be a consolation for that last-minute goal tonight."

The guys let out a collective "ooh" at the burn while Nyberg shook his head with amusement and downed the rest of his drink

"You know what? I'm gonna take you up on that," he said, throwing an arm around my shoulder and directing me toward the bar.

When the bartender looked over at us, I held up two fingers. "Can we get two Heineken?"

Passing over a ten as the bottles were slid toward us, I waved at him to keep the change and knocked the neck of my bottle against Nyberg's in cheers before taking a swig.

"You know," Nyberg started, "you played great out there tonight. Even though the whole team knew your style of play, the guys still had trouble keeping a read on you, and I'll admit, I was expecting you to take that last shot instead of passing it off."

"And that's exactly why I didn't."

He nodded in understanding. "But yeah, it's like you somehow honed your skills and changed your game while still being the strong center you've always been. It shows, and I think the move out west spurred it."

In the chaos of switching teams, moving, and getting my footing with the Royals, I hadn't realized that my game had changed or evolved. There hadn't been any time to even consider it. But he was right. I'd gone to Los Angeles with something to prove—with a fire burning inside me to show not just the Knights, but the country, that I was a valuable player. That I could help bring home a cup. And I'd done just that. I'd put my head down, studied, integrated into the system of play the Royals used, and had absorbed all the advice I could from my new coaches.

"Thanks, man."

"In other news though," he said, quirking a brow, "how did lunch go with Lia?"

"Good actually." I chuckled lightheartedly. "Really good."

There was a gleam in his eyes as he asked, "Afternoon delight good?"

"No." I shook my head. "But I took your advice and put everything out there. Told her about Chelsea, how I felt about relationships in the past, and how, even though our situation sucked, that I liked her." I shrugged, playing it cool, though I could feel the corner of my mouth pulling upwards involuntarily. "And it worked."

"Which means...?"

"We're figuring it out," I admitted, "but I guess you can say we're together."

"Well I'll be damned," he said before leading me back to the rest of the guys. "Yo, Wellsley went and got himself a girlfriend!"

Mixed in with the guys whistling and making fake whipping noises, it felt like a dozen responses were thrown my way at once.

"Damn."

"Seriously?"

"That was fast."

Brookes cocked a brow in disbelief. "You're telling me you—the guy who is more or less allergic to relationships—met a girl in the weeks since you've left and already jumped head first into commitment?"

"I didn't meet her out west," I replied before backtracking. "Well, I guess I technically did, but not within the last couple weeks."

Understanding flooded his features. "It's the girl; the redhead. Lia." I nodded and he clapped me on the shoulder. "Well congrats then. I'm happy for you."

"Thanks, man."

"So, are you going to be dipping out of here early then?" Nyberg asked, nudging my side with his elbow.

"Why?" I mused. "You keeping tabs on me?"

"Unlikely," he said with a scoff, before gesturing around to the guys with his beer. "But we missed you."

There was a feeling of contentment as I watched my former teammates nod in agreement, and I did my best to ignore the prick of emotion that sprouted at the realization I wouldn't be seeing them again for at least a couple months.

"I've missed you guys, too," I said genuinely. "And don't worry, you've got me for a while tonight."

Chapter 18

I was awoken Sunday morning to two alarms going off simultaneously. One was mine, but the other I'd never heard before.

Bleary eyed and confused, I reached out to put a stop to the noise coming from my phone before rolling over to see Derrick doing the same thing.

Oh yeah.

After he'd met up with his former teammates at the pub yesterday, he'd made his way over to my place. Given that it had been passed eleven at night, you would've thought I'd have already wound down for the night, but no. I'd fallen deep into work mode after giving half my attention to the game's broadcast earlier in the evening, and I hadn't even realized it was that late until Derrick buzzed up to my apartment.

I'd answered the door scatterbrained, still needing to finish up the loose ends with the section of my report I was working on, and I'd asked him to hang out for a few minutes while I did so.

Only it didn't take me five minutes. It'd been quarter to twelve by the time I clicked the save button for the final time and turned to look apologetically at Derrick, who'd made himself comfortable on the couch.

"I'm really sorry about that," I'd said, chewing on my bottom lip nervously as I stood and moved to join him.

He'd lifted his arm to wrap around my shoulders and pull me close. "Don't worry about it."

"But I know you're only here for the night and—"

"Lia, it's really okay," he'd said softly. "I like watching you get so enthralled in your work. It's sexy." My lips curved. "Plus, I'm very much aware you're in crunch mode with your defense, so I'm not going to fault you for putting your focus there."

"I wish I could give you more though."

"You're giving me a chance... and that's enough for me."

And then he'd shut me up with a kiss. Filled with passion and longing, we'd made our way to the bedroom and fell between the sheets, exploring each other again like we'd gone months without one another instead of a handful of weeks.

I barely remembered when we'd finally fallen asleep, but now, watching him turn back to me with a crooked smile, I felt the same warm and tingling feeling coursing through my veins that I knew I'd drifted off with.

"So, I know why my alarm is set so early," he said as he played with a few loose strands of my hair, his voice still rough and groggy, "but why was yours?"

"I'm productive in the mornings, so I've been trying to squeeze in some extra time to work on my defense."

His fingers stilled. "Even on weekends?"

Taken aback slightly, I was hesitant as I nodded and said, "Yeah. Things are coming down to the wire, and with finals around the corner, I know I can't get everything prepared without putting in extra hours."

"Sorry," he said, shuffling closer to cut off my rambling with a quick kiss. "I didn't mean for that to come out like it did. I get it. Plus, your determination and love for what you do is one of the reasons I'm so drawn to you." I exhaled slowly, my lips curving as he trailed a hand down my side and left it resting on my hip. "I guess I'm just trying to sort through the next couple weeks in my head."

I felt my forehead crease as my brows drew together. "What do you mean?"

"Well, with this," he said, squeezing my hip. "With us. I totally get that you're at the finish line of your PhD with your defense coming up."

"It's not until the end of April, but I'm trying to be extra prepared," I chimed in before waving off my comment, urging him to continue.

"Okay, so you're going to be swamped come April, and if things don't totally fall apart these last four weeks of the regular season, the Royals are going to be locked into a playoff spot."

"You'll be in the playoffs," I said confidently.

"Thanks." He chuckled, leaning in to trail a line of soft kisses along my jaw. "But if that's true, it means we won't really have a chance to see each other once April rolls around." Pulling back, he pecked my lips quickly, and looked into my eyes. "And while phones are great, it's no consolation for the real thing, you know?"

I lifted my hand and cupped his jaw, his six 'o'clock shadow scratching my palm lightly as I traced my thumb along his bottom lip. "Trust me, I know."

A spark of desire flashed in his eyes. "Then I guess what I'm trying to get at is, I don't think I'll be able to find time to fly back out to Boston before the playoffs." My heart sank at the realization, because while I knew this dating thing would be tricky, it hurt to hear the reality of the situation out loud. "And if you've been working a lot on the weekends, then maybe this is a shot in the dark, but do you think you could find time to fly out west when I'm playing at home in two weekends?"

"I..." I paused, trying to find the words when the main obstacle came crashing to the forefront of my mind. "I don't think I can afford it, Derrick. When I visited my parents at Christmas, that was the first time in two years I'd flown out that way."

"I can pay for the ticket."

I sat up, holding the sheet up against my chest as I shook my head "I can't—"

"You can," he insisted, sitting up as well. Both his hands cupped my face and made sure our gazes were locked before he continued. "This isn't me using my money to buy you a new car or send you away on a spa weekend. I want to fly you out so we can spend some time together."

"I know, and I want that, I do."

"Then don't focus on the fact I'm the one paying for your ticket," he said, leaning forward so that his forehead rested against mine. "Focus on the fact that I'm doing whatever I can to make sure I find time to spend with my girlfriend."

His words had my heart doing backflips, which, if I was being honest, kind of terrified me. Maybe it was because I knew he was creeping behind my defenses. Maybe it was because it'd been a while since I'd felt this strongly for someone—especially when, until yesterday, I'd purposefully been holding myself back. After Derrick had unlocked the flood gates, however, my emotions had risen to the surface and there was no tucking them away again.

"I can't even begin to guess how much work you still have to do for your presentation, but if it's at all possible to take a few days—"

"Yes."

His eyes widened as I cut him off and a grin blossomed on his lips. "Yes?"

My own lips twitched upward, and I nodded. "I'll talk to my professor to see if I can take the Friday off, or work on the plane, but I'll see if I can make it work."

Because while I felt this immense pressure to put everything I could into my final defense, wanting it to be the best it could be, I also knew with the way I'd been working lately, I could likely afford to take a few days off.

"Great," he chirped, and I laughed. "Now," he drawled, falling back onto the mattress and tugging me with him, "I've got about ten minutes before I have to call an Uber and get back to the hotel."

"Oh?" I quirked a brow suggestively. "How do you suggest we spend that time?"

His lips brushed mine softly and his hands trailed down to my ass. "I'm sure we can think of something."

It felt different saying goodbye to Derrick. Like it was the trade deadline all over again, except for the fact that we weren't cutting the romantic ties between us this time. And because of that, it made things one hundred times harder.

After a slew of last second kisses before he jumped in the elevator, I was left feeling slightly off balanced, wondering what to do and how to feel. So I did the only thing I could think of—I put myself to work.

Numbers, words, and graphs danced through my head and onto the screen as I cranked out another section of my report, finally starting to see the bones of what I was working towards come together. And though I'd taken breaks throughout the day to run errands and tidy the house, when Derrick called later that night, I'd been shocked to realize it was already going on eight 'o'clock.

Clearly I'd found the distraction I'd needed.

But after hanging up the phone more than an hour later and looking back over the progress I'd made, I realized I was a lot further along than I'd thought. Yes, there were still a few more sections to draft, and a lot of things would need to be finessed further through edits and feedback, but I didn't need to be planning every second of my day around work.

I could afford to have fun.

Which included messaging Esme and Harper to ask if they were free to go to brunch the following morning, knowing neither of them would ever turn down a mimosa.

"So, what prompted the noon booze fest?" Esme asked after our waiter had dropped off our drinks.

I lifted a shoulder nonchalantly. "Does there need to be a reason?"

The pair exchanged a look. "No," Harper replied, "but after our chat last week, we figured we'd be seeing less of you until your defense rolled around."

"Well, I may have realized I've been putting in a lot more hours than needed these last couple weeks, so—" I raised my glass in a single cheer and brought it to my lips. "—I figured I could slow things down. You know, actually enjoy these next couple weeks before I have to start stressing about what comes next."

They looked at me as though I was a total stranger.

"Who are you and what have you done with our friend?"

A breezy laugh escaped me. "I haven't magically changed since you last saw me."

"Maybe not appearance wise," Esme said, "but something—" She waved her hands in circles in front of me."—inside you did. Because we know you're juggling a lot with your work and applying for permanent lecturing positions, and suddenly it's like..."

Trailing off, I saw the dots connecting in her head, though I kept my features neutral as I waited for her reaction.

"Wait a second," she continued, scandalized at the route her train of thought had taken, "did you hook up with Derrick again?"

Harper's eyes widened, her voice hushed as she asked, "Did you?"

The corner of my mouth twitched. "I mean, I wouldn't really call it a hook up, per se."

"What do you mean you wouldn't call it a hook up?" Esme rambled, both confused and excited. "If you guys ended up naked while he was in town, it was a hook up. Unless..." Her eyes narrowed, scanning me up and down as though she could easily find the answer. Though I decided to put her out of her misery and let my grin widen. "Oh my god! Shut up!" She leaned forward, finally dialing her words down to a whisper. "You guys are dating?"

I nodded, hiding my grin with my drink as I took a sip.

"Wait, seriously?"

"I mean, we're trying," I offered. "I know that his job brought him out west and is going to have him hopping all over the country, and he knows I need to put my attention on finishing my PhD, but we also can't deny that there's something between us that distance didn't fracture. It's definitely not a normal situation—"

Esme snorted. "No, I wouldn't call dating a famous hockey player normal."

Rolling my eyes, I let the comment bounce right off me. "It's not a normal or easy situation," I repeated, "but maybe it'll work out somehow. I'm hopeful that it'll work."

"Then we're happy for you, Lia," Harper said genuinely, and Esme agreed. "Especially because he seems to have gotten through to you about taking some time for yourself—which is great!"

"Lord knows we couldn't do it."

"Well, I was working through everything yesterday—"

"Which better be why you put off telling us about this relation-ship development for more than twenty-four hours," Esme cut in teasingly.

"Guilty," I admitted sheepishly. "But yeah, I was working yesterday and started planning out what I had left to do, only to realize I was actually ahead of schedule." I paused, debating on how to drop the next piece of news before coming right out with it. "Which actually works out well, since Derrick invited me out to Los Angeles in two weeks."

"He did what?"

Esme's eyes shone with mirth. "Oh my god, is this what your life is going to be like now? Flying out for weekends with your boo?"

"I don't know," I mumbled, feeling a flush span across my cheeks. "I mean, it's not going to be like, every weekend, but if this is the only way we can see each other when our schedules match up, then I'm not going to say no."

"She's just teasing," Harper said, nudging her girlfriend lightly in the side. "Don't worry, we get that things aren't the same in a relationship when you can't see one another." Because while they'd been together for years, I knew there'd been a time when Harper had worked abroad for six months that had really tested their relationship. "So hopefully you and Derrick can make things work."

Esme wriggled her brows suggestively. "And find some fun ways to keep the chemistry alive."

"Yeah," I sighed, "so do I."

Chapter 19

"We're beginning to make our descent into Los Angeles, so we ask that all passengers please return to their seats. We'll make another announcement with deplaning instructions once we land and are heading toward our gate."

Murmurings of excitement could be heard around me as passengers began to look out the windows and get the familiar thrill that came with traveling. In contrast, however, I was wringing my hands nervously in my lap, wondering if this was truly the best idea.

Was I actually doing this? Flying across the country to see my boyfriend, who I hadn't even known three months ago?

Yes, I was. Because somehow, this guy—this striking, confident, good-looking guy—had begun to chip away at my defenses to burrow himself into a small section of my heart.

Even across the country, he'd found creative ways over the past two weeks to convince me that giving him a true shot was in no way a mistake. There had been days when I'd woken up to sweet good morning messages waiting for me, phone calls and video chats nearly every night to catch up with one another despite the miles between us, and on the Monday after we'd made things official, I'd come back to my office after lunch to see a small bouquet of wildflowers waiting for me.

Which had made the conversation with my professor later that day an interesting one. Awkward for me and amusing for her. When I'd asked about taking a day off, she'd looked at me knowingly. "I'm assuming that has something to do with whoever sent you the flowers today?" she said, and when I nodded, a breezy laugh fell from her lips. "Lia, it's fine. You're ahead on your research, you don't have lab time scheduled, and you aren't missing any lectures. Everyone needs time off, so take those couple of days to recharge and come back ready to put the finishing touches on your defense."

And I'd taken her advice to heart, because for the first time since I started my PhD, I had left my laptop behind in Boston. The action had terrified the piece of my soul that was hellbent on being an overachiever and reaching my fullest potential, but I'd listened to the logical side of my brain as I left my apartment earlier this morning.

This weekend was all about spending time with Derrick, not staring at a screen for hours on end.

"In town for anything special?" my seat mate asked, clutching the arm rests tighter with each meter we descended closer to the ground. Likely a few years younger than me, she'd been fidgety for the majority of the flight, but I could sympathize with the nerves and anxiety she seemed to have coursing through her body.

I gave her a shy smile. "Just to visit my boyfriend for the weekend."

"Oh, that's sweet," she said, before grimacing as the wheels of the plane hit the tarmac and things got a bit rough for a few moments. She exhaled slowly once the airplane attendant came back on the speaker and we headed towards our gate. "I'm here for a job interview."

"What kind of job?"

"Software designer."

"Wow," I said, visibly impressed. "That's great."

She nodded, and whether it was because she was excited or nervous—or both—she launched into a spiel about how she was excited about the opportunity, as it was for a company that'd been founded by a group of women she'd looked up to in the tech industry all through her university career. And honestly, she had spunk. She was clearly thrilled at the chance she was being offered, and if she had the skills to back up ambition, she was sure to achieve a lot in her career.

"That's great," I said, offering her one final smile when we finally made it to our gate and everyone around us began to grow impatient. "And good luck, though I don't think you'll need it. I'm sure you're going to ace your interview."

She grinned. "Let's hope so."

Wishing her well as I grabbed my carry-on from the overhead compartment, I followed the line of people off the plane, pulling my phone out of my pocket as I made my way through the airport. Switching it off of airplane mode, a few texts came in from my friends that I'd missed before boarding, simply wishing me well, and two much more recent messages popped up from Derrick.

Hey, practice let out a bit late and I'm just leaving the arena now. Hopefully I'll still be there in time!

I must've beaten the traffic, because I just found a parking spot. Heading over to the arrivals at terminal 5 now. Can't wait to see you x

That second one had been sent only five minutes ago, so when I looked up from the screen as I turned the corner into the waiting area, I didn't expect to see him.

Yet there he was.

Leaning against a pillar off to the side, his hair was a bit un-ruly—still slightly damp and on the long side—but he was clean shaven, showing the strong jaw line that was typically hidden by stubble. Otherwise, he was the same man that'd left two weeks prior. Same soft, full lips, same crooked nose, and same alluring eyes that were continuously scanning the crowd in search of one thing.

Me.

When our gazes finally met, I felt my lips involuntarily twitch upward, and before I knew it there was a full-blown grin on my face and the two of us were moving toward one another, meeting in the middle.

"Lia." He exhaled, encircling his arms around my waist. I let my bag fall to the ground as he hugged me tightly against him and snaked my arms up around his shoulders. With his nose buried in the crook of my neck, I felt his mouth brush against my skin as he whispered, "I missed you."

A burst of lust and longing shuddered down my spine. "I—"

He didn't even let me return the sentiment before his lips were on mine, caressing and claiming. Making up for all the times we'd spoken over video chat the last two weeks, unable to physically be next to one another. His tongue swept slowly along my bottom lip before twirling with mine as I opened for him, realizing that we were in public, but not necessarily caring.

"Well, hello to you too," I breathed when he pulled back a few moments later. "And in case it wasn't clear, I missed you too."

"It was clear," he replied with a smirk, "but it's still nice to hear."

After another purposeful kiss, I was the one who pulled back, combing my fingers through his hair. "What?" I teased. "No hat or anything to try and disguise yourself?"

He chuckled, squeezing my hips affectionately. "This city's a bit bigger than Boston, and with all the celebrities around these parts, I've learned trying to blend in actually makes you stand out." And as if the universe wanted to prove his theory to me, a family with three young boys walked by, enthusiastically talking about the Royals last game while not sparing Derrick a glance. Lifting a knowing brow, he nodded inconspicuously their way. "See?"

"Now imagine if those kids knew they'd just walked past the newest all-star hockey player to come to Los Angeles. I bet they would've been kicking themselves for not getting your autograph."

"You really think highly of me, eh?"

"Of course," I said confidently, kissing his jaw before stepping back to pick up the bag I'd dropped. "And don't try to get all modest. I've seen some of your games lately—you've been playing great. Being traded might've sucked on so many levels, but for your game, I think it did wonders."

"Yeah, me too," he admitted slowly, as though he hadn't admitted that fact to himself yet. "But enough about hockey, that's not what this weekend's about."

"Oh?" I quirked a brow. "I seem to remember you telling me I'd be in the stands for your game tomorrow."

He pinched my side, causing me to yelp in surprise. "Okay, Mrs. Smarty Pants, let me rephrase: this weekend isn't all about hockey."

Using a finger to swipe a stray strand of hair behind my ear, he leaned in and said, "This weekend is about you, and trust me, I have some great plans."

His voice was like silk—soft and smooth—prompting warmth to bubble in the pit of my stomach as I felt goosebumps coat my skin.

"Well," I drawled, reaching for his hand to intertwine our fingers, "I'd love to hear about these plans. Especially the ones that involve only the two of us."

"I'm sure you would," he said, a knowing gleam in his eyes, "but I think our first order of business should be finding something to eat."

As if on cue, my stomach grumbled loudly, and I flushed in embarrassment as Derrick laughed. "What did you have in mind?"

"Sushi?" he offered. "There's a great spot a few streets away from my place that has an all-you-can-eat deal."

"Sold."

"Enjoying yourself?" Derrick mused as the waiter walked away, having just written down my third order of dumplings.

"Immensely." This place was like heaven. "These things are delicious," I said, picking up the last of the dumplings in front of me and plopping it into my mouth. It tasted so good that I had to physically hold back a moan of appreciation. "In fact, everything here is."

We'd ordered an assortment of everything to start: shrimp tempura, a sashimi platter, chicken teriyaki, spicy California rolls, eel, crab, salmon, and of course, the specialty pork dumplings. All of it had been devoured, and we'd re-ordered our favourites, drawing out our dinner as we caught up.

"I'm not gonna lie, since the guys told me about this place, I've probably ordered their take-out special like three times," Derrick said, snatching the last crab roll. "But I'll admit, eating in makes everything taste better somehow."

"Maybe it's just the company," I said jokingly.

"That could definitely be it."

I nudged his knee with my own underneath the table and rolled my eyes. "Have you been eating out a lot then?"

Nodding, his smile turned sheepish as he said, "There's a reason I didn't take you back to my place for dinner. I think all I have in the fridge are some eggs and maybe half a carton of milk, plus a few basics in the pantry."

"You've been that busy?"

He shrugged. "I probably could've found time to stock the kitchen, but it's felt like my schedule has been changing on the daily, and it's just me, so it's been easier to get take-out," he admitted.

"Not judging," I said, "though—" I dropped my gaze to the table, a small amount of guilt fizzing in my chest. "—am I adding more to your already packed plate by being here?"

"Not at all," Derrick was quick to refute, easing my worry as he reached across the table and rested his hand on top of mine. "The only two things I care about this weekend are hockey and you. Everything else can wait, because when I said I wanted to try this thing, I wasn't lying."

"Me neither."

"And since hockey can sit on the back burner until tomorrow's pre-game, you've got the spotlight."

"What an honor."

He laughed, leaning back in his chair after giving my hand one last squeeze. "So, what have I missed these last couple weeks? Any girls' nights go awry, or new scientific discoveries made?"

"Sadly, none of the above," I drawled, "but I did end up finally submitting my application for the lecturing job at Harvard opening up for the May semester."

Derrick's eyes widened, as did his grin. "That's great, Lia!"

"And," I bit my lip, trying to contain the flurry of excitement and nerves that coursed through me whenever I thought about it, "they let me know my official interview will be on Wednesday."

"This Wednesday?" he asked, and I nodded. "Damn, congratulations."

"Thanks," I said, a soft, shy smile blossoming on my lips. "I know I'm likely the underdog, because of my experience, but I also have an edge on others because I think I'm the only one currently working with the department that applied."

"They'd be idiots not to bring you on board," Derrick said reassuringly. "And I know I can't really be of much help with the knowledge side of things—Lord knows I don't have a doctorate like you're about to have, let alone a degree—but I don't have a game on Tuesday. If you need help prepping for the interview, I could ask you questions over video chat and try to get you into the right mindset."

"I might just take you up on that."

As my third helping of dumplings arrived at the table, Derrick took over the conversation, going into some of the team dynamics for the Royals that I wasn't privy to, as well as listing off a bunch of spots his new teammates had introduced him to across the city.

"It's crazy," he said. "I used to come down to Southern California a few times every year with my family when I was younger, and we'd hit up Los Angeles every now and then, but there are so many places that tourists don't know about. I've literally got a list on my phone as long as my arm of places to scope out."

"Anything good we could check out tonight?" I asked, finishing off the last of my food.

"You're not tired?"

I shook my head. "I had a nap on the plane. Plus, it's Friday night and I flew all the way out here to spend time with you."

"Well, there's this pop-up market tonight out in Malibu we could hit up if you're up for a bit of a drive," he suggested. "We can look through the stands, walk along the beach, maybe take a dip in the water."

"No need to convince me," I said, grinning as I leaned across the table and pecked him on the lips. "I'm in."

Chapter 20

"So, let me get this straight," Derrick started, brow quirked as he glanced back over his shoulder at me, "this guy you work with—"

"Miles."

"Yeah, whatever." He waved me off before flashing his fob in front of the entrance to his condo building. "He tried asking you out the week I left Boston?"

"He did," I confirmed. "But I shut him down. Esme and Harper always thought he'd had a thing for me for years, but I never saw it. We were friends, you know."

"And now that you're both about to go your separate ways, he's trying to get out of the friendzone?"

"Exactly."

"Well," he drawled with a smirk appearing on his lips, "if he asks you out again, just make sure to mention your big and strong boyfriend while you let him down easy."

"I think he's realized you're still in the picture, especially since you sent those flowers," I mused, though sincerity seeped into my tone as I reached out my hands and placed them on his lower back, leaning in to kiss the exposed skin on the back of his neck. "Which, thank you for, again."

"No need to thank me," he replied as we stepped on the elevator. Turning so that we were side by side, he threw his arm around my shoulder and dropped a quick kiss on my lips. "You deserve to know I'm still thinking about you even when I can't physically be there."

Not for the first time that night, I was both touched and pleasantly surprised at how thoughtful and attentive Derrick was as a boyfriend. Or just as a man, period. Yes, having dated for a few months already, I'd known he wasn't an asshole, but he had an unassuming sweet side. Like he was a closet romantic.

On the drive out to Malibu, he'd held my hand. As we strolled through the market, subtly keeping an eye on the sunset, his palm never dropped from the base of my back. When the sun had finally begun to dip below the horizon, we'd found a spot to sit in the sand, and he'd cradled me between his thighs with my back against his chest. We'd spent the time murmuring to one another, listening to the waves roll in and watching the colors dance across the sky.

And that was only tonight.

Over the last couple of weeks there'd been good morning texts, flowers, and so many other, subtle peeks into the kind of person Derrick was. All of them conflicting with the version of himself he'd described when telling me about the last relationship he'd been in. Which made me think it'd been his ex who'd depicted him as the bad guy, because besides the long distance—an unavoidable part of his career—he was the furthest thing from a villain that I could imagine.

Definitely much closer to a Prince Charming.

Fading out of my thoughts and back into the current conversation, I hummed suggestively. "Well, you're physically here now. Or since I came to you, I guess I am."

"That you are," he said, lust shining in his irises. "And don't worry, I have big plans for you tonight."

"Do tell."

The elevator dinged, and with my bag in his free hand, Derrick led me to the end of the hall. "It'll be better if I show you." His voice was low and husky, prompting a shiver to run down my spine at the insinuation. "But," he continued, unlocking his door and motioning me inside, "I want you to see the place first."

There was a prick of curiosity as I felt a crinkle form between my brows, wondering what he was itching for me to see. It wasn't like I was going in blind. When he'd been deciding which condo to rent, he'd sent me the links of the online walkthroughs and had taken my opinions, choosing one of the two I'd thought to be the nicest. Sure, the condos had been empty in those videos—nothing but hardwood floors and white walls—but how much could really change in just a few weeks?

Evidently, a lot.

The walls had been painted—one a darker green while the rest were a light gray—and even though Derrick had been hopping across the country for games, the place looked to be fully furnished already.

"Wow," I said, looking around quickly. "You've had time to get all this done since getting the keys?"

Dropping my bag beside the couch, he leaned his hip against the arm rest. "I may have hired someone Ruderman recommended to help me out."

"Smart," I remarked, and when he stayed silent, watching me intently, I knew there was something more to it. Quirking a brow at him, I saw the corner of his lip twitch before I took a closer look, my gaze arcing around the space. And that's when I realized the true reason behind his eagerness for my reaction. "You went with my décor suggestions?" I asked in awe.

I'd mostly been throwing out ideas and patterns I'd seen while scrolling through Pinterest over the years when we'd video chatted weeks back about how he was planning to decorate his new place. But I'd never expected him to take me seriously.

There was no missing the shelf of fake plants above the television, or the patterned throw pillows lining the couch. Then there was the liquor cart off to the side and the canvas up on the wall that depicted the Boston skyline. All random, off the cuff suggestions I'd made, yet they were all put to use.

Derrick nodded. "I've never really had an eye for all this stuff," he admitted, gesturing his arms around us. "And your ideas were good, so I may have passed them on to the designer."

The way he shrugged nonchalantly had my head spinning. In a good way. "But you weren't writing anything down when we were talking," I pointed out. "I was just spitballing."

"I've got a pretty good memory," he replied, tapping the side of his head with his index finger.

"Well," I trailed off, moving over to wrap my arms around his waist, "now I'm wondering what other ideas of mine were put to good use."

"The rainfall showerhead."

My eyes widened. "You're kidding."

"Nope, and I'll definitely make sure to be there with you when you first try that out," he replied with a chuckle. "Oh, and—" He leaned down so that his lips were brushing mine. "—you also might want to check out the master bedroom."

Pulling back slightly, I asked, "Why?" But then a lightbulb went off in my head, and I untangled myself from his arms before scurrying down the hall to see if my guess was correct. And it was. "No way."

I'd always been a fan of wall paneling and statement walls, and vividly remembered going on a tangent about one such picture I'd seen with gray washed, horizontal wood paneling. It'd been completely random, but now the wall behind Derrick's headboard looked almost identical to the one I'd been mildly obsessed with.

Turning slowly, I saw that he'd followed me, and was leaning casually against the door frame. His full lips parted in a grin that practically oozed sex appeal and had my heart beating overtime.

"You seriously took all my ideas," I breathed out, flattered.

"I did," he confirmed. "Besides, I don't see the difference in this and going shopping together, which would've happened if we lived in the same city and I got a new place."

"The difference is that I would've known about it and—"

"Would've probably tried to convince me to choose something different," he said, cutting me off as he moved further into the room so there was little to no space between us. Eliminating the remaining inch, he squeezed my hips and pulled me closer so that we were chest to chest. Looking down at me, there was sincerity in his features as he said, "But I didn't want anything different. I liked your ideas. They were fun and laid back, and I figured that if I could only have you here a few times a year, then having you unknowingly decorate the place was the next best thing."

"That's..." I started, though trailed off when I couldn't find the right word.

"Adorable? Crazy? Sweet?"

I huffed out a laugh, shaking my head in disbelief. "Maybe all of the above."

When our gazes locked again, the air around us crackled with tension, and the next second, my arms were hooked around his neck, drawing his mouth down to meet mine.

One kiss. That was all it took—knowing we were alone for the first time since the airport and there was a perfectly good bed less than a foot away—to fall back into the delicious pleasure that sparked each time we were together.

Except this time, nothing about it was soft or sweet. No, we were both needy to make up for the last two weeks. I twined my fingers through his hair and after palming my ass with both hands, he lifted me so that my legs were wrapped around his waist as we got situated on the bed.

By the time my head hit the pillows, my shirt was halfway off, and Derrick made quick work of finishing the job before his lips were back. This time on my neck, trailing down my skin hungrily, easily popping the front clasp of my bra open to free my breasts.

"You know you're fucking beautiful, right?" Derrick growled against my skin.

I didn't answer. Instead, I grasped the hem of his shirt and yanked it up, pulling it over his head before my hands returned to his skin. He shivered under my touch, and I felt the obvious ridge of his cock through his shorts as his own hands got to work on ridding me of the rest of my clothes.

Looking down to see him crouched at the end of the bed, his eyes flicked up to meet mine, appearing dark with desire as his tongue flicked out to trace a line across my waist from one hipbone to the other. A move that had my hips lifting involuntarily, as though a silent plea for more.

"Tell me what you want," he said, before dropping lower and gliding his tongue across my sensitive skin, pulling a moan from my throat.

"Honestly, this whole night has been foreplay," I admitted in a blissful haze, grasping at his biceps to pull him back up the bed. My mouth claimed his quickly in a kiss before pulling back. "I really just need you inside me. Now."

No further questions were asked as he quickly shucked the remainder of his clothes and swiped a condom from his bedside table. Over the next couple seconds, he rolled it on, propped a spare pillow under my tailbone, and situated himself between my thighs before gliding inside.

And the familiar feel of him was exactly what I needed.

With him on his knees—fingers digging deep into my thighs as he thrust his hips hard and fast, never slowing down—I couldn't reach him. So instead, while one hand grabbed at the comforter beneath me, the other cupped my breast, rolling the nipple between my fingers.

There was a sharp inhale from Derrick in response, and a mumble that was either a curse or encouragement as he leaned over me, forearms resting on either side of my body as he continued to move. But now, each time I swirled my hips in time with his, my clit got the friction it needed and the sensations building inside me were quickly beginning to spiral to the point of no return.

"Fuck, Lia," he said, almost as though his teeth were clenched to hold off the inevitable. "I missed you."

"I missed you, too," I managed to reply, silently begging to be brought over the edge.

And as he plunged deeper and harder, the pleasure shot higher, causing me to scream his name once, twice, three times over until my orgasm washed over me, drawing a low groan from Derrick as he came as well.

We collapsed together on the bed, breathing hard, and when Derrick left for a few moments to deal with the condom, he returned to find my eyes already fluttering shut with exhaustion.

"Time change finally catching up with you?" he asked, pulling the sheets up over us before cradling my body against his.

"Probably," I mumbled, cuddling closer.

I felt his fingers run softly through my hair, lulling me further to sleep. "I meant it you know," he whispered, lips against my forehead. "I really have missed you."

I could feel a smile forming on my lips, but I didn't have the energy to move, let alone open my eyes. And whether my response was vocalized or solely in my head, I didn't know, as I said, "Me too."

Derrick hummed appreciatively as he dipped his head to kiss my neck. "You're looking mighty fine this morning."

Laughing as his gaze caught mine in the mirror, I nudged him away playfully. We'd already spent too much time together in here this morning under that wonderful rainfall showerhead he'd had installed. "Thanks, but shouldn't you be headed to the rink for morning skate?"

"I'm going, I'm going." He held up his hands in mock surrender as I finished with the top knot I was forming. "I'll probably be back around one, and then we can go grab something for lunch."

He'd popped out to grab me a coffee and bagel from the end of the street to tide me over until then, because he hadn't been kidding yesterday when he said he had no food. "Sounds good."

"And…" he drawled, "I have a surprise for you before the game."

I lifted a brow. "A surprise?"

He chuckled, leaning in for one last kiss. "Trust me, you'll like it." Retreating from the bathroom, I heard him shuffling around, likely grabbing his duffle on the way to the door. "Call me if you need anything."

"I will," I replied, and when I heard the door slam shut, I knew I was left alone.

Which, to be honest, was a bit weird to think about, but I didn't let myself mull over it for long.

Without my laptop and my work to pass the time, I settled in front of the television and scanned the channels, finding a home improvement marathon to watch. After all, it was a guilty pleasure of mine, peeping into how other people decorated their space.

Time passed easily, and as the fourth episode began, my stomach began to growl lightly. I figured Derrick would be home soon, but just as I reached for my phone, the buzzer for the condo went.

Had Derrick forgotten his key?

Thrown by the interruption, I figured after a few moments that maybe someone had just buzzed the wrong condo. Then the buzzer went again.

Not knowing what to do, I hesitantly picked up my phone, gnawing on my bottom lip as I dialed Derrick.

Was this supposed to be my surprise? Was I meant to answer the door?

After four rings, someone answered Derrick's phone, but it wasn't him. "Hello?"

"Uh, hi," I said, flustered with the current situation. "Is, uh, Derrick there?"

"Yeah, sorry," the guy—someone I assumed to be his teammate—said. "He's just in the showers but left his phone out for one of us to answer if you called." There was some rustling on the other end of the line before I heard him yell, "Wellsley, your girl's calling!"

The buzzer went off again, and this time, I moved towards the entryway.

"Lia?" I finally heard Derrick's voice in my ear.

"Derrick, hi," I said. "Sorry for calling, but there's someone buzzing your condo and I didn't want to answer it, but they're being persistent so—"

"Lia, it's fine," he chuckled. "You can go ahead and answer it."

"You sure?"

"Completely. And I'll be home in about twenty."

"Okay," I replied, still feeling as though something was off as I hung up. When I pressed the button and spoke into speaker, there was no response, leaving me to think that, for a moment, whoever it had been had simply left.

That is, until there were three raps on the door.

Clearly whoever it was meant to be here.

Unlocking the door, I nervously pulled it open and was faced with not one, but two people. A pair who were around my parents age, and just as I was about to ask how I could help them, a spark of familiarity set in. It was the color of the man's eyes and the crook in his nose, as well as the soft smile on the woman's lips.

Any words I may have had immediately got caught in my throat as a terrifying realization set in.

These were, without a doubt, Derrick's parents.

Chapter 21

W hat a wild turn of events.

When Lia had called, my first thought was that my surprise for her had arrived an hour early. Which wasn't that big of a deal. Hopping in my truck, I headed for home, keeping an eye on my phone as I waited for a text to come through filled with glee and excitement.

Except what she sent me instead was a short sentence full of confusion.

Were your parents… supposed to visit this weekend?

The answer? No. Definitely not.

My foot hit the gas a bit harder the rest of the way to my condo, thoroughly thrown about this hitch in my plans. I'd talked to my mom two days ago, after landing back on the west coast, and she'd not given me one clue that her and my dad were planning to come down for a visit. She'd certainly mentioned wanting to come to a game since I'd been traded to the Royals, but nothing concrete. Not tonight.

Once I'd parked in my building's underground lot, I totally disregarded the elevator and hit the stairs. Climbing two at a time, I continued up until I reached the eighth floor doorway, ignoring the slight burn in my thighs after this morning's practice as I all but stumbled into my door, throwing it open with haste.

I heard my mom's voice trail off at the noise, asking "Derrick, is that you?" right before I skidded to a stop. There on my couch sat Lia and my mom, my dad taking the chair to the side, and it was an image I certainly hadn't expected to come home too.

It was strange, but not wholly unwelcome.

"Yeah," I replied, pausing to take a breath as my eyes flitted between the three of them. "When did you guys get here?"

My attempt at being nonchalant and confident didn't quite take despite my best effort, as I could hear the dazed tone wrapped around my words.

"Twenty minutes ago, maybe," my mom said, looking to my dad for confirmation. To which he nodded. "We had a free weekend and thought we'd come down to surprise you. To watch your game and see your new place." Her gaze settled back on Lia. "We didn't know you had company though, or else we would've called ahead."

Lia was quick to hop in. "Like I said already Mrs. Wellsley, don't even worry about it."

Her voice was confident and airy, but I didn't miss the message her eyes sent me as she glanced back at me. The what-the-hell-is-going-on look that had me nervously rubbing the back of my neck.

"Well, uh, I'm sure you guys already went through introductions, but Lia, this is my mom and dad, and mom, dad, this is Lia... my girlfriend."

My mom stood, laughing with amusement as she walked over to give me a hug. "Well, I'd hope so, considering she seemed pretty at home when she answered the door. But why didn't you tell us you were dating someone?" she asked, pulling back to pat me on the cheek. "Especially someone as smart and beautiful as Lia?"

Redness immediately colored Lia's cheeks and I felt my own embarrassment creep over me as I mumbled, "Mom."

"What?"

I sighed. "Nothing, it's just... new—this relationship. I wasn't going to mention anything until I was sure we could make it work, what with the distance and everything."

"Oh!" my mom responded, as though this was brand new information. She looked slightly guilty as she turned to Lia and asked, "Are you not from around here, dear?"

Lia shook her head. "I'm just out here for the weekend. I live in Boston, but I did grow up in San Francisco."

"Derrick too!"

"Yeah—" Lia's lips quirked upward. "—he's mentioned it."

My mom huffed. "Well now I feel like we're interrupting your weekend together. I'm sorry I didn't call first, I just thought—"

"Mom, it's fine, really," I said with reassurance despite the flurry of issues now floating through my head at their sudden appearance. "Though—" A sheepish expression formed on my face, knowing I'd have to come clean about my plans for the rest of the afternoon earlier than expected. "—we'll need to take two Ubers to lunch now."

Unsurprisingly, Lia's eyebrows furrowed with confusion. "What do you mean? We should all fit in one."

And as if they were given a perfect cue, the buzzer to my condo sounded.

"We will," I responded before pointing toward the door, "but they won't."

My mom's gaze turned back to me. "You had other guests coming?"

"I invited them," I hedged, moving over to buzz them into the building without using the speaker in an attempt to keep the surprise, "but they're really here for her."

My attention turned to Lia, whose eyes widened.

"M-me?" she asked, stuttering with surprise.

I nodded, watching as she stood up slowly, a frown creasing her forehead, and made her way to the door.

"What did you do?" she muttered as she passed by me.

"You'll see."

My parents' eyes were on me, wondering what the hell I'd done and what they'd walked into, but my focus was on Lia. Watching her face intently as she opened the door, looking out into the hall, curious as to what—or more specifically, who—she was looking for.

And I knew the exact moment the elevator doors opened to reveal her surprise.

Her mouth fell open and she jerked her gaze back to me, silently asking if this was for real. Which it was. "Oh my god!" she squealed at my grin before rushing out into the hall to greet her parents. "Mom! Dad! What are you doing here?"

As the three of them chatted quickly in the hall, I felt my mother's hand grip my elbow gently, turning my attention her way.

"You flew her parents out?" my mom asked quietly, surprise coating her words.

The corner of my mouth twitched upward. "I did," I replied. "Actually, you guys were probably on the same flight without knowing it."

She didn't respond right away, instead letting her eyes searched mine. Seeking. Assessing. It was only after a few moments that she hummed to herself, as though she'd uncovered a secret.

"What?" I asked warily.

"Oh nothing," she mused. "I just figured my boy would've told me he'd fallen in love again."

I rolled my eyes. "Mom."

"What?" She turned to my dad, who was still seated. "Joe, don't you agree with me?"

He shrugged, much more of a strong and silent type, unlike my mom. "If Derrick says he's not in love, then we don't have a reason to believe he's lying."

"Thank you."

"But," he was quick to continue, lowering his voice as he nodded out to the hall, "I do think that woman out there is one to hold on to."

"Well so do I. That's why we're trying to make things work despite living thousands of miles away from one another, but it's too soon for love. You're seeing things because you've just met her, but we've only actually been dating for a few weeks."

My mom lifted a brow. "And before that."

"We were seeing each other," I admitted, "but it was casual. Then I got traded and—"

"And..." my mom interrupted, reaching up to pat my cheek, "sometimes love comes around at the strangest of times. That doesn't mean it's not love; it just means it's harder to hold on to."

Left digesting her words of wisdom as she moved back to the couch, every part of my body was hyperaware when Lia brought her parents inside, looking at me as though I'd gifted her the world. Her eyes bright and filled with warmth, and there was no dampening the grin that split her lips.

It was a look that, if I'd been moving, would've stopped me in my tracks. Her beaming expression shot a spark directly toward my chest, and it dug deep, finding an ember of emotion that'd sat dormant for so long. So long that, in that crazy moment, I couldn't recognize it.

But I knew it wasn't love.

It couldn't be. Not yet.

"I don't know how you pulled this all off," Lia said with awe as she came into my bedroom later that night, dressed in pajamas and fastening her hair in an elastic.

Neither did I.

This morning, I'd thought I had planned everything to a T. The front office had found three open seats for Lia and her parents to enjoy the game from the stands, I'd booked a table at a popular restaurant down the street from the arena for them to eat dinner at while I skated warm-ups, and I'd gotten her parents a room at a hotel a five minute drive away from my condo, as they hadn't wanted to intrude further—their words, not mine—on my weekend with their daughter.

The moment my parents had been tossed into the equation, however, things turned on their head.

But I rolled with it.

Introductions were made, and weirdly, I found it comforting that the pressure of meeting the parents had been balanced on both our shoulders instead of just my own. And while she'd more or less been thrown into the deep end, Lia seemed to agree. Lunch had gone without a hitch—the time spent delving into stories old and new alike. About how Lia and I had met (the more PG version), where our careers were headed, and then hopping way back to stories our parents seemed keen to swap about embarrassing childhood tales.

All of which we sat through, laughing and enjoying the time we had with them.

And with the hour I had before heading back to the rink to prep for the game, I led everyone around my neighbourhood on foot, giving them a brief tour of the hustle and bustle of Los Angeles.

I'd also spent that time making last minute changes to my plans. I'd called the restaurant I'd booked for dinner and asked about adding two more to the reservation—which they accommodated, and I'd texted the assistant to the general manager of the Royals to make sure there was space in the family box, since it would've been next to impossible to find five seats grouped together in the stands so last minute. And there was.

So, when the time came, I'd left Lia with the keys to my truck and hopped in an Uber, hoping their night would go without a hitch as I turned my attention back to hockey.

Which proved prosperous given the fact I'd nabbed two assists and the Royals had gone up 3-2 on Dallas. And from the reaction the five of them had had once I'd met up with them after the game—cheering and seemingly at ease, still living off the high of the crowd—it would've been difficult to call the night anything other than a success.

Lia's reaction now only secured that.

"Like seriously," she continued, a smile unfurling, "today was amazing. Different and unexpected, but amazing."

"Well, I can't take all the credit." I chuckled, already situated in bed as I flipped up the comforter, inviting her to slide in and join. "My parents definitely weren't a part of the plan."

"Which is insane," she replied, shaking her head. "What are the odds that the one weekend I fly out, and you fly my parents out, is the same weekend yours decide to jump on a plane as well to surprise you?"

"If I could guess, probably very, very low."

"Yet you still rolled with the punches." She cracked a smile, turning so that our gazes were locked. "And I know I sound like a broken record, but I really did have the best day."

With a hand resting lightly on my chest, she leaned over and pressed a kiss to my lips. And there were no complaints from me. Gentle and slow, I let her lead, and despite the truly maddening rhythm, I didn't push further. Instead, I sunk into it, focusing only on her as I squeezed her waist and pulled her closer.

It didn't last all that long, however, and when she finally pulled back, her hand stayed centered on my bare chest, fingers moving slowly while her head fell into the pillow next to mine.

"In all of today's craziness, I never did ask," she whispered, "how did you even get ahold of my parents?"

"You have some pretty accommodating friends," I replied, my hand stroking her hip under the covers. "Esme told me the name of their restaurant and I rang them up once I'd bought your plane ticket."

"And they listened? To you?" she said with disbelief. "A total stranger?"

"I think your mom knew, despite you not mentioning me by name, that you'd been dating someone." Despite the lights being off, I could see the way her cheeks darkened with a blush. "Also, one of her customers had asked her about a picture of the two of us that'd ended up online."

Her eyes widened. "What picture?"

"I never looked," I replied honestly, "but there's going to be pictures out there. They'll never be front-page news, but if I've learned anything the last couple years in the league, it's that some fans like to have a bit too much information about our personal lives."

"That's... so strange."

"Agreed."

"They can't have moments like this though—" She cuddled closer. "—right?"

"No," I trailed off, "they can't have this."

No response followed; only a few long moments when neither of us said a word. Yet, I felt every curve of her body against mine. Every time her chest fell and rose against mine, and when her lips finally brushed against the corner of my jaw, my hand drifted upward to cup her breast.

Only for her to pull back with amusement glittering her irises.

"Sorry to disappoint," she drawled, "but as much as I'd like to get naked with you right now, it's not happening with your parents in the next room."

"Damn," I breathed. "Cockblocked by my own parents."

A soft chuckle escaped her. "They leave a few hours before me tomorrow." She craned her neck to kiss me. "I'll make it up to you before I fly out."

Those words should've been the cause of a cold shower, prompting my mind to run off in one hundred creative directions, but tonight, they didn't. Not when the suggestiveness was overshadowed by the fact that she was indeed flying back east tomorrow. Because her life was out there, and mine had brought me across the country.

And for the first time, I was hit in the face with the downside of this weekend. That three days with her was simply not enough. However, there was no ace up my sleeve, and nothing I could do to stop her from leaving.

So, I did all I could. I tightened my arm around her waist and pressed my lips against her forehead.

"I'm holding you to that."

Chapter 22

The weekend in Los Angeles had been a whirlwind. I'd spent less than seventy-two hours on the west coast, and somehow had managed to squeeze in a hockey game, quality time with both my boyfriend and my parents, as well as a handful of little adventures around Derrick's new city.

Not to mention all the sex.

But sadly, the fairy tale came to an end all too quickly, leaving me to settle right back into life in Boston.

"Are the two coffees a good thing or a bad thing?" Harper asked when I took a seat across from her and Esme Monday morning.

"Neither," I responded, taking a long gulp to try and get as much caffeine flowing through my body as possible. In an attempt to prolong my weekend with Derrick, and because there'd been limited tickets left so last minute, I'd taken a red-eye back from Los Angeles and had only landed a few hours earlier. I'd been so close to canceling, but after realizing I had no coffee at home, I knew there was no way I could get through the day without it. "Just precautionary, since I didn't really sleep all that well on the flight. So, I'm hoping this—" I shook the coffee cup in my hand slightly. "—can get me through the day until I can crash in my own bed."

Esme lifted a brow, an ounce of concern noticeable in her expression. "Was it just the plane that made it hard to sleep? Or was it knowing you were leaving your man on the west coast?"

And if I was being honest with myself, it was mostly the latter.

Typically I was okay with flying overnight, or as good as any normal person could be seated in coach. Last night, however, I couldn't get my brain to shut off. I'd close my eyes and think about the weekend Derrick and I had shared—the nights wrapped up in one another and the days spent laughing and exploring—wondering when we'd get a chance to be in the same time-zone again.

Looking down at my cup, I asked, "Does it being the second one make me a fool?"

Harper shook her head. "You couldn't be a fool even if you tried."

"Apparently I can be," I said, "because I used to be logical about things like this. How the hell is anything about my relationship with Derrick logical?"

"Logic doesn't always come into play when it comes to love, Lia."

My shoulders fell as I blew out a long breath, that simple four-letter word floating around my head. "He flew my parents out guys."

The words tumbled out with whispered awe, and while it wasn't a new revelation, I'd been too busy enjoying my time with them to fully digest the significance of the action until now.

Both of them feigned shock and I rolled my eyes.

"I know you guys helped him pull it off," I said, watching as their expressions turned sheepish, "but I still can't believe it happened. Like, how did he even come up with the idea?"

"Did you ask him?" Esme asked, lifting a brow. "Because he didn't give us much information when he looped us into his plan."

"I did."

"And?"

"He said he wanted to make the most out of my visit. That he was thinking of a way to make me feel at ease with taking time off work and also didn't want me sitting all by myself in the stands at his game. And despite how crazy it'd sounded, he'd thought finding a way for me to see my family was the perfect solution."

"Are you doubting him?" Harper asked.

I shook my head. "No, no, it's just... who does that? I've never had a guy do something that thoughtful. And obviously he had the means to do so, but it wasn't even about the money. It was the fact he happily gave up time that was supposed to be about the two of us to give me some rare time with my parents. And that was before his family showed up."

"I'm sorry—" Harper blinked, suddenly confused. "—what?"

"Oh, yeah, did I forget to mention that his parents also decided to surprise him by flying down for his game?"

"Damn girl," Esme said, "so the weekend ended up being a whole family affair?"

"I mean, not the whole time." I felt a blush creeping up my cheeks, thinking of the hours we had to ourselves. Something that didn't go unnoticed by my friends, who both shot me knowing looks, though stayed mum. "Most of the day Saturday was spent together and they all flew out around noon yesterday, but because of Derrick's game, I had to ride things out without him for a few hours."

"And how was that?"

"Honestly... it was okay," I admitted. "I obviously hadn't expected it, and had kind of pumped myself up to be cheering in the stands alone, but it wasn't as awkward as I thought it'd be. His parents were super sweet, especially his mom, since his dad was definitely more on the quiet side, but my parents also helped fill the silence. And then at the game, we ended up being led to the box with other families of the players."

Harper's eyes widened. "No way."

"Way." I took a long gulp of my coffee. "There were wives and girlfriends, and other player's kids. And to be honest, it was a little intimidating at first. Once the game started though, most people turned their attention to what was happening down on the ice."

"Well, just be glad this all happened out in LA," Harper said, "because if you were getting that VIP treatment when he'd been playing for the Knights, I might've grown insanely jealous. Or bugged you to take me along to all the games as your plus one."

"Ditto," Esme added, and I laughed.

"Since when does a plus one get a plus one? Or two?"

"We would've figured it out," Harper mused before her features softened. "But since we don't have to worry about that... we just need to know that flying out there was worth it."

"It was worth it." Flashes from the weekend replayed in my head. "Definitely."

The only downside?

That after a weekend where Derrick had managed to wiggle his way even closer to my heart, we were almost three thousand miles apart, and I had no idea when we'd be able to see each other again.

That first week back in Boston had been a big one for me, with my interview for the Harvard lecturer position barreling toward me all too fast. I'd been buzzing with nerves, but keeping to his word, Derrick called me on Tuesday night after an afternoon game—the first of three on the team's south east road trip. His voice alone had managed to settle my mind, and in the hours that followed, he acted as a sounding board, listening while I went over details of the job, my qualifications, and sample interview questions. It was extremely helpful, and come the following day, it'd paid off.

Sitting in front of two members of the department whom I'd met sporadically over the course of my studies, I'd appeared confident and knowledgeable. Like someone who was ready to step into this role and knock it out of the park.

And clearly they'd thought so too, because I'd been told a few days later that I was moving on the final phase of the hiring process. It included various faculty members sitting in on the last few lessons of my undergraduate class, watching and making notes as I wrapped up the material, which was stressful. Any time a student raised their hand, I had a small panic before they spoke, wondering if I'd be able to properly answer their questions or clarify the material, but I'd gotten through it.

Which left me in a holding pattern, waiting for the department to evaluate the other candidates before they came to a decision. So, I reverted my focus back to my defense, because even though it wasn't an official part of the hiring process, I had a feeling they'd wait until they saw my presentation before I received an answer.

Making it all more important for me to nail it.

Though I did make sure I didn't let it take over my life. I still saw my friends, talked to my family, and, despite the time difference, managed to keep my relationship with Derrick alive and well.

We never went a day without catching up, whether that be over text or FaceTime, and when I got the news I'd made it further in the interview process, he'd sent me the most beautiful bouquet of flowers. So, when the end of March rolled around and the Royals managed to snag a guaranteed spot in the playoffs, I figured I needed to repay the favor.

And what was the equivalent of flowers for men in a long-distance relationship?

Phone sex.

It'd been completely new to me, but once the idea of it popped into my head, I'd gotten a thrill at the notion of trying it.

Derrick hadn't known what I had planned, and when he answered the FaceTime call, only to see me in a new lingerie set, his jaw had damn near fallen to the ground. Though his surprise didn't last long. Wide eyes quickly filled with lust, and through the entire experience, he'd been patient with me. Using his deep, compelling voice to instruct me to move like he wanted—slowly and laid out for his viewing pleasure—getting us both off after a tortuous build up.

And after finally hanging up, there was a redness to my cheeks as I bit my lip, coming to the realization that I'd actually gone through with it as the aftershocks of pleasure coursed through my veins.

Evidently my body had thoroughly enjoyed the experience, because when the next day came, I still felt like I had an extra spring in my step as I walked into the office I shared with Miles.

"Morning."

He sat at his desk, riffling through a freshly printed stack of papers, only turning at the sound of my voice. "Morning," he replied with a tentative smile.

I quirked a brow. "I take it you're nervous?"

Wearing a pair of navy slacks, a white dress shirt, and a blue patterned tie, he exhaled slowly, relaxing back into his chair. "A little," he admitted. Today was the big day for him. In less than twenty minutes he'd start presenting his defense to a few selected members of the department, and I was planning to sit in the back of the room as a silent cheerleader. After all, we'd worked together and leaned on one another in a work sense for the last five years, and it only made sense to be there for him now that it was all coming to an end. "I've been over this presentation so many times, I have it memorized, but while I've tried to come up with an answer to any possible question I could get asked, I'm still expecting a curveball or two."

"You're going to do great," I said encouragingly.

Rubbing his hands together, he said, "Let's hope so." Collecting his papers, he slipped them into his messenger bag, along with his laptop, before slinging the strap over his shoulder. "You coming?"

"You go ahead," I replied, "I'll follow in a few minutes. Room 1025, right?"

He nodded. "Just don't be late."

"I won't be."

As he left to go set up, I opened up my email and typed out a few quick responses to students who'd reached out for help on the problem set I'd assigned the day before, but before long, I was logging off and making my way downstairs.

The sign asking for total silence was already taped to the door, though it was still ajar as I slipped inside, giving Miles one last reassuring glance before the last professor entered the room. With everyone accounted for, I took a seat in the back corner of the room and watched the presentation commence.

While the concepts behind Miles' research were explained, I momentarily flashed back to the two of us watching a defense in this very room at the end of the first year we'd spent working toward our doctorate. Not unlike the two students on the opposite side of the room. Like them, we'd both been thrumming with nerves, still feeling out of place, yet wide-eyed at the confidence and poise the presenter spoke with.

And now it was our turn to step up to the mantle, with Miles going first.

Listening as he veered into his experiments, learnings, and theories, he spoke with conviction while still showing both sides of the coin—the good and the bad. The professors at the front were jotting down notes as the hour-long presentation went on, but otherwise appeared incredibly enthralled by his work. Just like I was.

That is, until his presentation began to wind down. He'd laid out all his conclusions and was going over next steps when some phrases he used began to sound oddly familiar despite having not seen this part of his work.

Then a bomb dropped in the pit of my stomach.

The end of his presentation wasn't just familiar, it was stolen. From me.

All the extra work I'd put in over the last month to connect both our areas of study—the experiments, the time spent correlating results, the conclusions—they were being used to prop up his own work. To convince the panel of professors he'd been the one to start this work that would propel the faculty forward.

When really, it had been me.

Sitting in the back, no one could see as my face drained of color at the realization. No one except Miles, and he didn't seem like he gave two fucks in that moment.

Not wanting to cause a scene, I held my tongue and began to squirm, trying my hardest to keep my emotions in check despite the flame of betrayal hollowing out my chest. It was crushing to know that Miles would do something like this. Making me think that, while it'd been one-sided, even his interest in me over the years was a front for his hidden agenda. He didn't like me, he liked my brain, and wanted to capitalize on it any way he could.

Which either made me an idiot, or him the most manipulative person I'd ever met.

Gritting my teeth through the entirety of the question portion, watching as he had a response for every question thrown at him, my shock turned to anger. How could he do this? And how did he even get this information? I hadn't yet finished the draft of my report or presentation with my new work, so the only way he would've found it would've been if he'd been on my computer. Which, considering I rarely locked my screen over lunch or when I left the office, was, unfortunately, a real possibility.

What an asshat.

When everything was officially over, I couldn't get out of there fast enough.

Heading back to our shared office, I knew I couldn't be here when Miles returned, because I was almost positive I'd lose my shit on him. So, I sent an email to Professor Klein, telling her I wasn't feeling well and was heading home—though having listened to the presentation, it wouldn't take her long to connect the dots around the true reason I was leaving.

With next to no traffic and my mind a capsule of chaos, I felt like I'd made it back to my place in no time. After all, it was only eleven.

Oh, how the day could change in just a few short hours.

Letting the front door slam shut, finally in the sanctuary of my own home, I let the lid off my bottled up emotions, and while the anger was still there, the betrayal and hurt rushing came back with a vengeance. Making a beeline for my room as the overwhelming feeling washed over me, I curled into a ball on my bed. My face was pressed into my knees as silent tremors shook my shoulders, and I let the tears fall.

Knowing that the one person I wanted to lean on was the one person that couldn't be here.

Chapter 23

While some coaches eased up on practices and conditioning after landing a spot in the playoffs late in the season, the Royals certainly didn't. Sure, if someone wasn't feeling one hundred percent—whether that be a new injury or old—they'd sit out, but getting the best seed possible was just as important as getting into the playoffs in the first place.

Which meant that as the season wound down, I was watching game tape with my new teammates, hitting the gym for longer than normal, and working with the offensive coach after practices on ways to even better amalgamate myself with my line mates.

It was hard work, but hopefully it'd pay off in the form of a Stanley Cup come June.

But before that, there were still three more regular season games to play, and since the team was flying up to Edmonton early tomorrow morning, Coach had more or less instructed us all to relax tonight. For the first time in over two weeks, I was ready to leave the arena before five 'o'clock.

"Yo, Wellsley," Quinn said, stepping out of the showers with a towel wrapped around his waist. "You up for pizza and video games at my place in an hour?"

Having already dressed, I nodded, digging through my bag for my phone. "Sure, man. I'll just—" I paused as I glanced down at my phone, which had been tucked away all day, to see two back-to-back phone calls from Lia around eleven this morning. And considering we mostly texted while she was at work, a bit of an uneasy feeling slithered into the pit of my stomach. "On second thought, I might take a rain check on that."

He lifted a brow. "Everything okay?"

"I'm not sure," I replied, raking a hand through my damp hair. "I have a few missed calls from Lia this afternoon, so I'm gonna head home and try to get a hold of her."

Another one of my teammates nudged me playfully in the side. "What'cha do that could've got you in hot water?"

"Nothing."

At least I was pretty sure I hadn't done anything that could've upset her.

"Don't worry," Quinn said, shoving my other teammate away to clap me on the shoulder. "I'm sure it's nothing. Or she could just be struggling with the long-distance thing. What's it been, like two or three weeks since you've seen each other?"

"Going on three, yeah."

"Then if it's anything, and I'm not saying it is, she probably just had a spare minute at work and was missing you."

"You should take this one's word on it," Ruderman said, jumping in as he passed us on the way out of the locker room. "After all, he's been tangled up with a woman in Texas for three years."

"I'm telling Bree you said that," Quinn mused, watching as Ruderman shrugged and waved goodbye.

"Your girlfriend lives in Texas?" I asked.

"Fiancée," he corrected.

"No shit."

He chuckled. "Some of the guys give me shit about it, especially because, other than a handful of weekends and holidays, we only really see each other on the off season. But we've made it work. Besides—" He shrugged. "—I know I'm not going to be in the league forever, she has a great job, and I know that she's the one for me. Every relationship is different, and when things are long distance, it just means communication is all the more important."

As I nodded, he moved to his locker to get change while I packed up and headed out to my truck, wondering if Lia and I's relationship was on the same path as Quinn's. Not that we were anywhere close to an engagement, hell no, but if the 'living-apart-for-years' path was the only avenue for long-distance relationships when both people had careers they were passionate about, then what did our future hold?

Would we be playing phone tag with one another for years to come? Or never be able to physically be in the same city, or even on the same coast, when one of us needed the other? Would we miss birthdays? Could I... could we... be in a relationship that was second string to the rest of our lives until we could devote more time to one another?

Was that fair to me? To her?

The whole way back to my condo, I had one foot on the gas and the other tapping anxiously along to the radio, and my hands were clenched around the steering wheel. I didn't like the thoughts swirling around my head. Not one bit. And for a moment, wished I'd left the locker room a few minutes earlier. If only I had, I might've missed Quinn's views on long-distance.

Because while they worked for him, I wasn't sure they worked for me.

By the time I reached my place, my mind was a mess, and when I pulled my phone out of my bag, I saw another missed call from Lia.

Collapsing on the couch, I raked my fingers through my hair as I called her back.

She answered on the third ring.

"Hello."

"Hey you," I drawled. Just the sound of her voice had a small weight lifting off my chest.

If she were here, I imagined myself wrapping my arms loosely around her waist, my hands skimming over her ass while I pulled her body closer. Then I'd dip my head and kiss her smile, content in enjoying the company and affection of the amazing woman that stumbled into my path—quite literally—a few months back.

Instead, I sat alone, waiting to hear her speak again.

"How was your day?" she asked after a few moments. "I'm guessing things were busy?"

I hesitated with my answer, noticing her voice had taken on a monotone note. "They were," I said cautiously, "but are you okay? I saw you'd called a few times this afternoon. Did something happen at work? Are you sick?"

My chest tightened when her dry, tear-filled laugh traveled over the speaker. "How can you do that? How can you just tell that something's wrong?"

"Because, babe, I've been paying attention," I replied softly. "I'm going to hang up and call you back with video."

I heard her say 'okay' before the line went dead, and I quickly opened FaceTime, clicking on her name from my recent call list.

Once the call connected and her face popped up on my screen, her distress was even more evident. She was laying in bed—which, after yesterday, should've been something that got my gears going—but it didn't. Not one bit. Instead, I wished I could jump to the east coast, because she was wearing pajamas, blankets wrapped around her, hair piled messily atop her head, and her eyes were on the red side; cheeks stained with tears.

But despite that, I noticed she tried to muster a smile.

"Hey." My voice was soft and gentle, hopefully a source of comfort for her. "Do you want to talk about it?"

I didn't know what'd happened, but it was clear that something had caused her day to go up in flames.

"You remember Miles?" she asked, a hiccup punctuating her words.

I nodded. "Yeah..."

"Well," she started, sniffling before launching into a recount of her morning. How it'd been Miles day to present his defense to the department and she'd gone to support him. How he'd done a great job and seemed to really impress everyone in the room. And then, how he'd somehow gotten a hold of her latest research findings. How he'd used the work she'd spent the last month on to end his presentation on a high note, and how she'd been so taken aback that, as soon as she could, she bolted from the room.

"What the fuck?" I asked, my nostrils flaring as anger bubbled in my veins. "That's complete and utter bullshit. Can he get away with that?"

"I don't know," she replied, her chin quivering as she burrowed further in her blankets. "I-I don't think so, but the idea for that research sprouted after reviewing his results in the first place. He could claim that it was an extension of his own work."

"Did anyone in your department know what you were working on?"

She nodded. "Our supervising professor did," she replied.

"Well, then she can confirm the work was yours, right?"

"I hope so, but I didn't get a chance to talk to her before I left." Her voice cracked, and tears began to fill her eyes. "My thoughts were going haywire and I couldn't take the chance that he'd come back to our office because I honestly might've lost it on him."

"Which is fair," I said. "You shouldn't have to deal with him, Lia. That guy's an asshole."

"And to think, everyone always thought that he was into me." A bitter laugh escaped her lips. "Now we know that he was just using my friendship as a way to exploit my work and push himself further ahead."

The blunt sarcasm was a sharp contrast to her whispered words of anguish, and it felt like a hand was tightening around my heart watching her sadness shift to anger.

It threw me back to the middle of February, when the rumors surrounding my trade were ramping up. When I'd been closed off and infuriated by the hand I'd been dealt. How the team that'd truly built up my career had all but thrown me out with the trash when I was no longer of use to them.

Only her situation was worse because she hadn't seen the betrayal coming.

And I couldn't be there for her like she'd been for me.

"I'm sorry," I said softly. "I don't really know what to say to make you feel better, or if I can say anything at all. I just wish I was there with you."

"Except you're not."

Taken aback by her directness, I was stunned speechless, and watched as her eyes widened once she realized what had slipped out.

"I'm sorry," she whispered, squeezing her eyes shut for a moment. "I'm just frustrated and—"

"Lia, it's okay," I cut in. "I want to know when you're upset, even when it's with me."

All of a sudden, the thoughts surrounding Quinn and long-distance relationships—which had been slowly making their way to the back corner of my mind—were once again front and center. Devilish and haunting, warping my ability to think clearly.

"But look," I started again, carefully trying to search her features before sighing, "if you're having regrets about us..."

"About us?" Lia repeated. Her forehead creased and a shot of surprise flickered in her irises. "Why would I be regretting us?"

I must've looked like a deer caught in a set of headlights as I stammered through my response. "Isn't that what you were saying? That you're upset I can't be there for you?"

"No, Derrick," she said sharply. "I'm emotional because Miles could've fucked up everything I've worked hard for over the last five years. If I can't rely on my latest research, then my defense won't be nearly as strong as it could've been, and if I don't nail it, the department can easily choose another candidate for the lecturing position. I'm upset and worried about my career, but now you're telling me I should also be worried about this relationship between us not working out?"

I flinched at her words. "That's not what I meant."

"Then what did you mean?" she asked. "Because it sure sounded like you were suddenly having second thoughts about long-distance being able to work."

"I'm—"

"Does it suck that you're not here right now? Sure. But I knew that would be a part of this going in. And I thought you did too, considering you're the one that brought up the idea of continuing to see one another despite the fact you're now based in Los Angeles."

"I did know that."

"Yet I still vividly remember you also saying that your last relationship failed because your ex thought you couldn't balance your feelings and the distance. And maybe she was right." Those words hurt like a shot to the chest. "Clearly you still have some deep-rooted issues about being able to handle a relationship, so maybe you should get those sorted out before trying to offer your shoulder for me to cry on."

There was nothing left for me to say, mostly because she clearly didn't want to hear it. Disconnecting the chat from her end, my phone screen went black, and I was left looking at the guilt seeping into my expression.

Tossing my phone aside, I groaned loudly, leaning forward as I combed my fingers through my hair with frustration. Because if there was one thing I knew for certain, it was that I'd royally fucked that up.

Chapter 24

When I woke up the next morning with a headache pounding behind my temples, I definitely didn't feel any better. In a span of twenty-four hours, I'd managed to ride a truly horrific emotional rollercoaster. From elation and pride, to betrayal and heartbreak. There was a high possibility of the day being written off as the worst I'd experienced thus far, and the fact that I was meant to continue on as though I wasn't a jumbled mess of a human seemed completely implausible.

I tried though.

Rolling out of bed, I sluggishly got ready for the day, ignoring any and all texts that came in, not wanting to take the chance of seeing Miles' or Derrick's names pop up on the screen. Because if I had to relive yesterday's events before I even gulped down my morning coffee, there was a good chance I wouldn't make it out of the house.

Instead, I drowned everything out. Putting my headphones in, I scrolled through the playlists saved to my phone until I found the one filled with throwback jams and turned the volume up. There was no room for unwanted thoughts while classic lyrics invaded my mind.

When I pulled into my usual parking spot at the university an hour later, however, I couldn't bury my head in the sand any longer. I needed to at least work to settle one of the storms in my life and deal with Miles. After all, there was no avoiding him. We shared an office. However, being that it was Thursday, I had one final class to teach before finals started, which meant I had a few hours to psych myself up and plan how to go about the confrontation before it happened.

Though with the amount of questions my students had, I didn't really get a chance to do either.

Riding the elevator up on the way up to the office, I couldn't help but fidget. My foot was tapping impatiently, and I fiddled with the zipper on my bag, taking a deep breath as the doors opened and I stepped out. Heading down the hall, I felt like a young kid walking toward their parents, knowing they were in trouble, when I should've been feeding the rage inside of me.

But I wasn't a confrontational person, and a situation like this was honestly one of my worst nightmares.

Biting my lip, I silently chanted "You can do this. You can do this."

Only to open the door and see an empty office.

Truly empty—at least on Miles' side.

My side remained untouched, but on his side, only the desk, chair, and computer monitor remained. There were no papers sprawled across the desk, no sticky notes lining the side of the monitor, and no books piled off to the side.

Setting my bag on top of my own desk, my forehead crinkled with confusion as I took a seat, looking around for a clue as to what had happened. Before I could jump to any conclusions, however, footsteps sounded in the hallway, and moments later, Professor Klein knocked on the door.

I straightened in my seat. "Good morning, Professor."

"Morning," she replied, and it wasn't hard to miss the tightness in her jaw. Or how her response failed to confirm the morning was indeed good.

I gulped, casting my gaze downward. "Professor, I—"

It was clear there was nothing I could say to stop the direction this conversation was headed, as she raised her hand, cutting me off. "Lia," she started firmly, clasping her hands in front of her, "I realize yesterday's events may have been overwhelming and cause for an investigation, but I wanted to let you know, before you heard elsewhere, that the department has decided to not look into the conclusions and next steps Miles presented in his defense."

Those words, while upfront and honest, put an ache in the back of my throat. All that work, down the drain. Completely and utterly useless now.

"But why?" I asked, my voice strained, needing to understand. "I realize there needs to be solid proof, but we both know he stole my work." My fists clenched as a wave of anger rolled through me. "I came to you weeks ago about this and you had first-hand knowledge that I was the one working to prove if my hypothesis was correct. I have lab results saved under my name for the past month. I don't get how, even with that knowledge, the department would decide not to investigate his actions."

"Because, Lia, with technicalities at play, Miles didn't steal your work."

I sent her a blank look, baffled by what she was saying. "W-what?"

Taking a seat in the empty chair, she looked me in the eye and explained. "While he used his presentation to make it appear like the work was his own, everything was properly cited in the appendix slides, and when I questioned him about it once you'd left, he didn't deny that you'd been the one to do the actual work. He said that framing the next steps of the research for the department was important, and that he figured since you'd already begun work on it, if he touched on your latest results, we would be more inclined to see that the work he'd done over the years was being used to continue our research. Was it ethical? No. But was it against university policy? Also no."

"So, if there aren't any consequences to what he did, then what happened to all of his things?" I asked, a crinkle of confusion on my forehead as I motioned to the empty side of the room.

"Well, I wouldn't say there were no consequences to his actions," she replied. "While we've deemed his defense successful, we have strongly suggested he remove the material he took from your research from his final report that'll go on to be published. He's also been given an unofficial warning for his actions from myself and the rest of the panel yesterday, and his application to continue working with this department has been denied. He'll be finishing up what's required of him to receive his doctorate and then he'll be moving on.

"As for his things, I know you're still moving full steam ahead with work for your upcoming defense, and that his actions yesterday had an effect on you. So, for the remaining duration of his time here, Miles will be working in an office two floors down."

I could feel my eyes widening the more she spoke, but the final point caused my brows to lift with surprise. "Seriously?"

She nodded with affirmation.

"You mean—" I felt a bubble of hope grow in my chest. "—this didn't damage anything in regard to my work? I can still present my research?"

"Of course you can," she confirmed with a light laugh, and it felt like a weight had been lifted from my shoulders. "Was that what you were worried about?"

"Kind of," I replied sheepishly.

"Lia, I thought you were simply angry about Miles actions."

"Oh, trust me, I was," I admitted, relaxing back into my chair as I expelled a breath. "But I was also worried that all my hard work had gone down the drain because of him. My mind raced to the worst-case scenario and believed that Miles had ruined both my defense and my chance at the lecturing position."

"Well, I can safely say that you don't need to worry about any of that," she replied with an encouraging smile. "Your work has been fantastic over the years, and this new research of yours has really given a lot of faculty members hope our work will continue to be successful for years to come. From what I've seen so far, your defense should be solid, and as for the job, I believe they'll be coming to a final decision in the next couple of weeks, but I'm rooting for you. I want to see you stick around."

The corners of my mouth ticked upward. "Thanks, Professor. That means a lot."

"It's well deserved," she said before standing. "But now that that's been said, I hope you're breathing easier."

Nodding, I said, "I am."

"Good, then I'll get out of your hair and leave you to your work." As she stepped into the hallway, she turned back to look at me.

"And that anger you may still have at the situation with Miles? Use it. Let it fuel your way forward to prove to everyone that you belong here. Because I'm expecting great things from you, Lia, and I know that you're capable of delivering them."

I couldn't find the words to respond as an overwhelming feeling washed over me. Knowing that someone I considered to be my mentor believed in me was one of the best feelings in the world, and with my worries about Miles cast aside, there was a desire inside of me to make Professor Klein—and myself—proud.

So, with a renewed sense of confidence, I spun around in my chair, logged into my computer, and I got to work.

The high only lasted so long though.

While I was incredibly productive during the hours I spent at work, as soon as I got in my car and began driving home, all my other problems came rushing back to the forefront of my mind. Specifically, the fight between Derrick and I.

He definitely hadn't helped the situation by fueling my already emotional brain with the fact that he was clearly questioning our relationship, or at least the distance part of it, but I knew I was also somewhat at fault. In my frenzied state, I hadn't taken the time to let him explain himself, because if I had, I'm sure things might've ended differently. It wasn't like I found our unfortunate relationship situation to be a walk in the park. Hell no. But instead of listening to him, I'd let my rage boil over and had said some absolutely awful things to him. Things I truly didn't mean and now felt insanely guilty about.

And the worst thing was, I didn't know if a simple apology could fix what'd been broken.

I needed a second opinion, and seeing as I had yet to tell Harper and Esme about the fight, I figured my mom was the best option. After all, she gave the best advice. Plus, there was zero chance for her being able to drop by to try and console me when all I needed for that was a pint of ice cream.

Hence, when I got home, I changed into a pair of sweatpants and an oversized sweater before sluggishly walking back out to the living room. I plopped myself down in the middle of the couch with my phone and dialed my mom's cell.

Being a weekday and only around three 'o'clock out west, I assumed the restaurant was in the lull period before the dinner rush began, as she answered on the second ring.

"Hey, honey," she greeted, and I could hear voices in the background for a moment before they stopped. Presumably because she walked into the back office and closed the door. "Is everything alright?"

There was no hiding anything from her.

"Well, actually," I started, my voice hesitant as I tried to figure out the right way to spin this, "I need your advice."

"Okay... on what?"

"Derrick and I may have had a fight last night—"

"Oh, sweetie. About what? The distance?"

"Mostly, yeah," I sighed. My heart ached as I launched into a play-by-play of the conversation we'd had. And this time, she didn't interrupt. I imagined her sitting in her office chair, nodding along to my explanation and taking everything in. "I know I was the one who brought up the fact he wasn't there for me, but I was frustrated with the situation, and then it all just spiraled from there."

My mom was quiet for a moment. "Well, it's been, what, three weeks since you've seen each other?"

"About that, yeah."

"Then my guess is you're both starting to really feel the pressure of being apart for the first time. Before you both knew when you'd be seeing each other next, but now that there's this unknown in front of you, you're both hyperaware of it."

"Which makes sense. Except I'm scared that what I said yesterday will make him throw in the towel," I admitted, my voice cracking. "I haven't heard from him since."

"I've only met him once, dear, but I'm a pretty good judge of character, and I don't think Derrick would end things because of one fight."

The problem was, it wasn't just the fight. The distance was the main issue, and it wasn't something that could be pushed under the rug.

"Then what can I do to fix things?"

"I think it's rather simple, Lia," she said. "Do you love him?"

My eyes bulged at the simple question, but with the way my skin tingled and my heartbeat began to race, I knew the answer.

"I do," I finally whispered, admitting it out loud for the first time, "but it's not realistic."

"Sometimes love isn't realistic, Lia, but that doesn't mean it isn't real."

"I just don't know how things can work out with us being on opposite ends of the country."

"If he means that much to you, you'll find a way to make it work."

Except, it turned out, I was a scaredy cat. A wimp. A big fucking chicken.

After talking to my mom, I took a few days to get my thoughts together, which gave my friends ample time to figure out that something was off. And when they finally intervened to drag the truth out of me, I was smothered with love, empathy, and a lot more opinions.

Harper thought I should be the first one to reach out, whereas Esme was adamant I wait for him to extend an olive branch. But I couldn't choose.

I couldn't find the right words and didn't know how I could both erase what I'd said in the heat of the moment and take a step toward a solution to our problems with the distance.

So I said nothing. I put all my energy into work and tried to push my relationship problems to the back of my mind, and before I knew it, over two weeks had passed without a word from Derrick.

I was deep into my pit of avoidance.

The only problem was, I had two friends who were die hard Knights fans. Which meant for years I'd gone over to their place during the playoffs to cheer on the team, and even though I knew they'd understand if I decided to bail, I didn't want to do that.

Besides, watching the game included drinking alcohol, which I could really use.

It turned out not to be so bad, seeing as the man I didn't want to think about no longer played for the team, but things went downhill south near the end of the third.

I was blissfully unaware of most of what was going on, content on chatting and enjoying the company of my friends on a Friday night, but I knew when Harper turned her attention back to the television screen and suddenly went silent that something was wrong.

"What is it?" I asked.

"Um, you might want to take a look."

Brows furrowed, I glanced at the TV, not seeing anything amiss with the game. The Knights were up by two goals in the fifth game of the series, and a win tonight would put them in the lead. But when my gaze dropped to the bottom of the screen, I saw it.

The Royals had played the sixth game in their playoff series tonight, except things had not gone so good for them. They'd lost and had officially been eliminated from the playoffs.

"Shit."

Both of my friends looked my way. "What are you going to do?"

The opposite of what I had been doing, because I couldn't ignore Derrick anymore. Not when I knew how much hockey and the playoffs meant to him, especially after the rollercoaster of a season he'd had.

Pulling out my phone, I still didn't know exactly what to say, but I figured starting off simple was a start.

I'm sorry.

And after waiting hours, my heart sunk to see that while the message had been read, there was no response.

Chapter 25

T he season was over—at least for the Royals—and it was bittersweet.

I always did look forward to the time off after every season, because after working my body to its limit week in and week out during the season, having a handful of months off to recharge and simply relax always did wonders. However, this season, the vacation came earlier than I'd hoped.

Especially after the chaos these last couple of months had entailed.

I'd started the season off as a Knight, had worked my hardest to stay, and had still been traded. And while I'd thought I'd landed with an overall stronger team—the players meshed well together, the coaching staff was tough but fair, and our penalty kill was one of the highest rated in the league—I was now on the sidelines while my old team made a run for the cup.

And I was happy for my old teammates, I was, but I was also jealous. Because if things had been different, I could've been next to them on the ice, riding the playoffs out together.

Instead, I was in Los Angeles three days after our game six loss, cleaning out my locker until training camp started up again.

Having already thrown my equipment in the back of my truck, I was just grabbing the extra workout gear I'd stored at the rink and the junk that'd accumulated over the last two months.

"Hey," Ruderman said, clapping me on the back as he walked into the room. "How's it going?"

I lifted a shoulder, zipping up the duffle that I'd brought with me. "Could be better," I replied honestly. "How are you taking the loss?"

"It definitely sucks, but I also know there's nothing that we can do to change it. At least this season." He smiled encouragingly. "Next season though, man, we're going to work hard to get that cup."

"You know it," I agreed, and the two of us fist bumped.

"So, what are your plans for the off-season?" he asked, taking a seat on the bench next to my bag. "Seeing family? Sticking around? Heading back to the east coast?"

I rubbed the back of my neck. "Honestly, I haven't thought much about it. I'll probably go see my folks for a few weeks, but other-wise, I've got a place here, so it doesn't make sense to head back to Boston."

While a handful of guys had already booked their flights back to their home countries for the next couple of months, the rest were set to scatter across the states in the coming weeks. Ruderman and his wife, however, lived in the Los Angeles area full-time, and it seemed like me, him, and two or three other guys were the only ones planning to stick around.

He looked slightly shocked by my answer though, raising a brow. "You're not going to try to fix things with your girl?"

"Uh..." I trailed off, not knowing what to say. "I'm not sure there's much I can do."

"As long as you didn't cheat, which I know you didn't, there's always something you can do," he said. "I know you've been zeroed in on the season the last couple weeks, and I totally get it, but hockey's over now. And didn't you say she texted you after the loss?"

I had indeed.

The message that'd come through was just two simple words. I'm sorry. Yet those alone, with the added heart as punctuation had made me yearn to hold her.

But then the regret and embarrassment settled in, knowing I'd compartmentalized my life after the fight Lia and I had, and put my focus solely on hockey. I hadn't reached out to try and mend things, because I really hated the idea of not being able to do so in person. I didn't have the ability to hop over to Boston for a weekend, and I knew she didn't have time in her schedule to fly out here either, so I'd done nothing.

The fact that she'd also not tried to contact me had me thinking that maybe I'd made the right choice, but then her text had come through in the exact moment I'd wanted to hear from her, and suddenly, I felt like my choice was the wrong one.

And now I didn't know what to do.

"She did."

"That was an olive branch, man. The ball's in your court to fix things, and you have time off, so hop on a flight. Go get your woman."

I couldn't stop the way my lips twitched upward as I rolled my eyes. But truly, I was thankful for his advice. "Aren't you going to be lonely if I jet off to Boston?"

"I think I'll manage," he said with a chuckle.

After a moment, I sighed, raking my fingers through my hair. "You think she'll even talk to me after the silent treatment?"

"If she ever had true feelings for you, trust me man, she will."

She will. She will.

About an hour later, after I'd hit up a taco truck for lunch with Ruderman, I pushed through the front door of my condo with three bags full of hockey gear. Letting the two duffle bags full of workout clothes and under armour drop to the floor with a thud, knowing they definitely needed a wash, I rolled my equipment bag to the hall closet and tossed it inside.

After all, I wouldn't need it for the next couple of months.

Shutting the closet door, I sighed, once again hit with the melancholy feeling that went hand in hand with the end of the hockey season, but as I moved into the living room, I was also hit with an unexpected bout of loneliness.

Realizing that I was in a city where I knew next to nobody (except a few of my new teammates) for the next few months didn't sit well with me, and honestly, made me restless.

Almost as though he could tell I needed a friend, my cell rang, and I pulled it out of my pocket to see Nyberg's name flashing across the screen.

Sinking into my couch, I let my head fall back against the cushions with a groan and answered the phone.

"As much as I love you as a friend, I really hope you didn't just answer the phone while rubbing one out," was the first thing Nyberg said.

I snorted. "Not likely. I don't need your ugly mug in my head while I'm doing that."

"Well, I figure that the long-distance thing must be tough on you. And now that you have a lot of time on your hands, maybe don't moan when answering the phone," he teased. "You don't want people to get the wrong idea."

"I'll keep that in mind," I said slowly, tapping my hand against the couch as I realized I hadn't told him about what was going on with Lia. Which meant that, apparently, I wasn't just a bad boyfriend from a distance, I also wasn't that good of a friend. Great. "But listen—"

"So, how are things with your team?" he asked at the same time, and I let him speak. "Is it the same kind of somber, after-season lull that happens over here?"

"Kind of," I replied, raking my fingers through my hair. "It's definitely the same routine. You know, a couple meetings about facility access during the off-season and preliminary plans for training camp. But I'm feeling better this year knowing the Royals are planning to keep me around. Last year, I spent most of my vacation waiting for the trade call."

"I remember. But that's good; you can relax and enjoy the time off."

"Yeah... wish I was still in the race for the Stanley Cup though."

"You guys will come back stronger in October."

"Says the guy still skating," I mused, and he chuckled. "I am rooting for you guys though."

"We definitely have a tough road ahead, but we'll see where we land. I'm hoping for June, but you never know." Spoken like a true player in the off-season, not wanting to jinx their chance at taking it all the way. "Be sure to let me know when you're back in Boston though. We gotta catch up."

And we were back to the elephant in the room.

"I'm actually on the fence about coming back to Boston," I admitted.

"What do you mean? Aren't you coming to visit Lia?"

"Um, we actually broke up," I said. "At least I think we did."

There was silence for a moment before a few curse words slipped from his mouth. "Why didn't you tell me, man? I wouldn't have mentioned her."

"It's fine, really."

"Clearly it's not," he said. "And what do you mean you think you broke up?"

"We had a fight a few weeks ago and haven't really spoken since."

"A few weeks ago?" he repeated, flabbergasted. "What the hell happened?"

Sighing, I spoke dejectedly as I recounted the events of the dreaded phone call. How sad and heartbroken Lia had sounded after Miles betrayed her. How she'd called me out for not being there for her. How I'd stupidly brought up the uncertainties surrounding the long-distance part of our relationship at the exact wrong time. And then how things had fallen apart from there.

Nyberg whistled incredulously once I finally finished. "Wow. And you guys haven't talked since?"

"No, not besides a text she sent after we got kicked out of the playoffs" I replied. "At first, I didn't know what to say, and then I figured if she wanted to talk, she'd reach out, so I focused on hockey." A dry laugh left my lips. "Though a lot of good that did."

"I hope you don't hate me for saying this, but while I get where you were coming from, you definitely should've reached out after giving her a day or two to cool down."

"Yeah," I trailed off, groaning inwardly as I dragged a hand down my face. "I know I messed up."

My heart and mind had raged against one another in the days following the fight, but unfortunately, the latter had unfairly won out. I figured I could only do so much from the west coast, that the Royals needed my undivided attention, and more importantly, because it had stung as one day turned to two and two day turned to two weeks without hearing a word from Lia.

"I mean, imagine if what'd happened to her had happened to you. I don't think you'd exactly be in the right frame of mind."

And dammit, he had a point.

"Ruderman suggested I call her and try to clear the air, but what do you think I should do?"

"Smart guy," he remarked, "but you shouldn't be taking advice from others, man. You just need to ask yourself what you want to do."

I exhaled slowly. "I want to fix things, because dude, I'm pretty sure I'm in love with her."

"Then maybe don't try to mend things over the phone, considering your last conversation went downhill that way," he suggested before pausing. "Look, the Knights are heading on the road to start the second round of the playoffs tomorrow afternoon, and we'll be gone for four days. And you're on vacation, so, if you really think there's something between you and Lia worth salvaging, then maybe this is the time to come back and see if you guys can make it work. Feel free to squat at mine for a few days too if you need to figure out how to make your move."

Everything inside of me was screaming to take the advice. To go. Yet the one thing holding me back was the embarrassment I felt about how I'd handled this whole situation. Because everyone knew that love was a gamble—that there was no guarantee you'd win—but I hadn't just lost. I'd taken myself out of the game.

But I couldn't let that hold me back. I needed to apologize and get over my doubts about long-distance. I needed to fight for Lia.

Plus, remembering that she was set to present her defense to her department in just two days' time, I knew just the way to do so.

"Nyberg, I might just take you up on that."

Chapter 26

I wiped my hands on my trousers and took a deep breath after looking over my notes one final time.

Today was the day. I was presenting my defense to Harvard's Bioengineering department. Five years of hard work, research, and perseverance had gone into this degree, and if all went well today, I would officially be receiving my PhD when commencement rolled around in a few months' time.

Butterflies fluttered around in the pit of my stomach, but I tried my best to keep calm. I'd spent five years studying and working towards this moment. I knew what I was talking about and could, realistically, recite my presentation in my sleep. I was that well-rehearsed. I just needed to believe in myself.

After all, I had a support system of friends and family who'd all sent over encouraging messages this morning. A myriad of good lucks, well wishes, and you're-gonna-knock-it-out-of-the-parks. And if they believed in me, there was no reason I couldn't do this.

With only fifteen minutes left until my defense was set to start, I gathered my things and headed downstairs to the room I was set to present in. As the first one there, I continued to shake out my nerves, tapping my feet in a not-so-rhythmic beat, as I moved about and set up my laptop, but as the five-minute countdown ticked by, people began to file in.

Professors from the department, two colleagues I'd worked with over the years, and a few other students who took seats at the back of the room.

Thankfully, Miles was nowhere to be seen.

As the clock struck ten, one of the professors who'd interviewed me for the lecturing position straightened the papers in front of him and said, "Whenever you're ready."

I nodded, grabbing the remote control from the desk at the front as I expelled a slow breath. Turning to face the room, I saw Professor Klein give me an encouraging smile as she, along with the rest of the panel, waited for me to begin.

"Thank you, Professor," I started, before addressing the rest of the room. "And thank you all for being here. Today, I'm here to talk to you all about my research around artificial cell generation, specifically surrounding the different methods available to us for transplanting hand-crafted genomes into living cells, as well as the pros and cons to each method."

With each slide came new information; words I'd memorized to show the professors in the room just how familiar I'd become with my work. And when it came to the data, I let the numbers and charts speak for themselves. Using a laser pointer to draw their attention to the clear facts on my slides, I briefly explained the trends and outcomes, making sure not to overwhelm them with information.

I was clear and concise, gaining confidence as the minutes ticked by.

Before I knew it, I was wrapping up my presentation, recommending the same next steps to the department that Miles had just weeks ago, except I had the additional data to back it up.

"And that's why I believe, using the last method I presented before you here, there is an evident pathway to explore full synthetic cell generation. The artificial cells held their structure when subjected to my preliminary metabolic tests, and this department has the resources to expand this research into a more comprehensive strategy toward the end goal." With those last words, I took a deep breath and smiled at the room. "Any questions?"

Given that they'd all been jotting down notes while I'd been speaking, it wasn't a surprise when questions began flying my way. They asked me to expand on certain parts of the research or clarify a slide that had been slightly confusing, as well as explain how I'd decided which steps to take during my experiments and how my processes had begun to yield successful results. Then they'd asked how I'd come to hypothesize the method for fusing my artificial cells with optimal metabolic tests, which brought me back to the day, weeks ago, when I made the discovery in the first place. How I'd rushed to Professor Klein's office as my mind raced, though I left that detail out when I gave my answer.

"Well, I must say, this has all been very impressive, Lia," the lead professor said when there were no more questions. "If you wanted to step into the hall for a few minutes, the four of us will deliberate and let you know the verdict."

"Thank you," I said with a nod as I turned on my heel and headed for the door.

The moment I stepped out into the hall it felt like a weight had been lifted off my shoulders. Leaning back against the wall, I exhaled slowly, in disbelief that it was really over.

But it was. I'd done it. I'd absolutely crushed it.

The minutes spent waiting felt long, but soon enough, the professors emerged from the room, offering me kind words as they passed and headed back to their offices, leaving Professor Klein to deliver the news.

"Well?" I asked, hope filling my chest.

Her lips lifted into a smile. "You passed."

I had to stop myself from slapping a hand over my mouth as a squeak escaped. And then another, more excited one.

Professor Klein laughed at my reaction. "Congratulations, Lia. You truly deserve it after all the hard work and dedication you've put into your studies these last five years."

"I couldn't have done any of it without your guidance though, so thank you."

She shook her head. "You would've excelled anywhere, and with anyone as a mentor, because that's just the type of person you are. Which is why I'm honored to say the department has decided to keep you around for a little while longer."

I inhaled sharply, surprised. "You mean—?"

"You should check your email when you return to your office," she replied knowingly, "but I'd like to be the first to congratulate you on your new position here at the university."

Oh my god!

I internalized most of my excitement, trying to remain professional, but I couldn't help the beaming grin that appeared. "Thank you."

"You deserve it," she said. "But do remember you still have exams to get through and a report to hand in, so don't celebrate too hard just yet."

While she was right—there was definitely still work to be done—there was no way I was letting this weekend go by without a bit of celebratory champagne. "Understood."

Going our separate ways, I quickly re-entered the classroom to collect my things before heading for the elevator. And once the metal doors closed in front of me, I let the elation inside of me go. Jumping in frenzied movements, I shimmied my hips and squealed with glee, letting the reality of what'd just happened sink in.

I'd passed my defense and landed the lecturing position.

What a day.

Composing myself as the elevator dinged open, I walked down the hall toward my office, patting my hair down as I went. Though the smile on my lips was not disappearing.

That is, until I noticed the door to my office was cracked open and the light was on. Two things that were definitely different from how I'd left them. And I swear to god, if Miles had decided to show his face, he would be regretting it momentarily.

But as I pushed the door open fully, it wasn't Miles that was in my office. No. My breath whooshed from my lungs when I saw Derrick hop up from my chair.

"D-Derrick?" I stuttered with surprise.

I blinked, wondering if what I was seeing was a dream. An illusion of some sort.

Nope, he was actually here.

Derrick shoved his hands into his front pockets, his shoulders tense as a small, meek smile pulled at his lips. "Hey."

I felt my heartbeat speed up as I asked, "What are you doing here?"

There was a wink of silence before he answered, and during that time, my eyes flicked to my desk to see a small bouquet of pink tulips resting there.

"Well," he started slowly, "I knew today was your big day and I wanted to be here to cheer you on. Though once I got here, I figured an outsider wouldn't exactly be allowed to watch a defense, so I thought I'd catch you after the fact." He gestured to the flowers. "These are for you by the way." Analyzing my expression, however, had him suddenly frazzled, given that I had yet to give him any indication that my defense had been successful. "Unless, shit, Lia, did things not go great?"

My resolve cracked slightly as my lips quirked upward. "I passed."

A subtle spark of joy lit up his eyes. "That's great," he chirped, bringing up his arms as though to give me a hug. He stopped mid-movement, however, thinking better of it and cleared his throat to cut the awkwardness. "I mean, uh, congratulations. You must be relieved it's over."

"It's definitely a burden off my shoulders," I admitted, "but I still have a few things to do before I'm completely finished with my degree."

He nodded in understanding before dropping his gaze to the ground, letting a lull of silence dance between us. Long enough for it to start becoming uncomfortable.

"Look—"

"Derrick—"

We both went to speak at the same time, and were quick to bite our tongues once we realized we were talking on top of one another.

"You go," Derrick said.

"Okay, well, I was just going to ask why you were really here," I said. "Because while I don't doubt you remembered today was my defense, you live in Los Angeles. A text or phone call would have sufficed, and after a couple weeks of not talking—which I know is just as much my fault as it is yours—I can't imagine it's a coincidence that you're back in Boston."

I needed to know, because there was a strong urge inside of me to do away with the space between us. To put my arms around him and fall into his embrace as though the weeks since our last conversation hadn't happened.

Except they had. This was the first time in weeks that I was hearing his voice, and while I couldn't blame him for vanishing and turning his focus elsewhere, since I'd done the exact same thing, we needed to talk.

Derrick sighed before meeting my gaze. "I'm here because I miss you. I miss talking to you about my day and seeing your smile, even if it was through my phone. I miss hearing you talk about your work and helping you study. I just miss you. When the Royals got knocked out of the playoffs a few days back, the only person I wanted to talk to once the night was over and I was alone in my condo was you."

"I tried to be there for you though," I pointed out. "I reached out that night."

"I know." He raked his fingers through his hair, grimacing. "When I saw your text come in, there was a part of me—a large part—that wanted to respond. To talk to you about how much it sucked the season was over, but I also didn't want to just sweep our fight under the rug. And I wanted to be able to apologize in person.

"I'm sorry," he continued with sincerity, taking the smallest step forward. "I'm sorry that I brought up distance being an issue with our relationship, because while it did suck to be far away from you, it wasn't a big enough issue to make things fall apart completely."

"But you weren't the one to bring it up," I said, fidgeting with my hands. "I was."

"You tried to apologize after that first outburst though," he countered, "while I was in my head. I'd just talked to a teammate about his long-distance relationship, and I'd been thrown by the fact that he'd spent three years with his fiancée and only gets to see her a few months a year. It had me thinking that was the direction we were heading, and after not seeing you for a couple of weeks, I was getting down on myself."

"And if I'd let you talk, you would've told me that, and I would've understood," I said, and it was true. "I was upset and emotional and I immediately directed my anger toward you."

"How did that whole situation go by the way? Did Miles get what he deserved for stealing your work?"

"By a technicality, he didn't steal my work." I rolled my eyes, still of the mindset that he did, in fact, steal my work for his own gain. "He credited me in fine print and didn't deny it was my work when questioned by the department. So, he passed his defense, but he definitely got what was coming to him. The department is letting him go, which means after he hands in his final report, he's done with this research team."

"Good riddance," he mumbled.

"Yeah, I won't have to worry about running into him this summer."

It took Derrick a moment to realize what I meant, but when he did, his eyes widened. "You mean you got the lecturing position?"

I nodded, unable to keep the smile off my lips as I thought about it.

A cheery laugh escaped him, and I didn't stop his movements as he wrapped his arms around my shoulders and pulled me into his chest. His happiness reinvigorated my own and I found myself grinning into his shoulder, closing my eyes as my hands drifted slowly up his chest, landing on his pecs.

"Congratulations, Lia," he said, pulling back and lifting a hand to my cheek. Rubbing his thumb softly against my cheek, he continued, "I know how much you wanted it."

"Thanks," I replied softly.

Looking into his eyes, seeing the sincerity of the man I'd fallen in love with, it was impossible for me not to lean forward. The feeling of his mouth was familiar, even with the barely there contact.

"Wait," Derrick said, leaning back once more. "I need you to truly understand how sorry I am about the lack of communication these last couple of weeks."

"You don't have to apologize anymore, Derrick," I said. "I did the same exact thing. I turned my focus to my work, and I can't fault you for it."

"And while that's great to hear, because I also don't fault you, I want to say that I do think we can make our relationship work. Long-distance isn't for the faint of heart, but if it's the only way to keep you in my life, as my girlfriend, you bet your ass that I'm going to do it. And when I get the schedule for next season, I'll immediately sit down with you and try to figure out every possible chance we have to see one another."

My hands smoothed down his chest. "You'd do that?"

"Of course," he said, as if it was the easiest question he'd ever have to answer. "After all, I seem to have fallen in love with you, so I definitely don't want to let you go. If you'll have me, that is."

A feeling of euphoria washed over me at his words, leaving me beaming up at him. "I love you, too," I said, unable to think of any other suitable response, and before I could get another word out, Derrick's lips were on mine.

For real this time.

The way our lips moved wasn't tentative or soft; we were hungry for one another. I used my teeth to nip at his bottom lip, prompting a moan, and in return, his tongue delved into my mouth, tangling with mine, reigniting the sparks that seemed to always flow between us.

When I tipped my head further to the side, not even thinking that we were currently in my office, his mouth trailed down my jaw and found the spot beneath my left ear that always seemed to light my body aflame.

Bringing my hands back to his cheeks, I fused our mouths together once more, indulging in hot kiss after hot kiss until I finally pulled back, breathing hard.

"How long are you in town?" I asked, my cheeks surely flushed pink.

"Well," he replied with a smile, his fingers tracing the soft skin just beneath the hem of my shirt, "I'd planned to stay long enough to apologize and win you back. Then I figured we could make a plan together."

"You don't have any other plans for your off-season?"

He shrugged. "I mean, not really. I'd like to see my parents, maybe find my way to a tropical island, but I know for a fact I want to be with you, for however long you'll have me."

I quirked a brow. "Are you saying you want to move in with me for the summer?"

We hadn't known each other long—it hadn't even been four months—but the possibility of having him around for the foreseeable future had my heart loop-de-looping inside my chest. It was a risk, but it was one that felt right.

"It depends," he trailed, "is that something you're comfortable with?"

Grinning up at him, I nodded. "I think I'd like that."

"Well then—" He leaned down to peck my lips. "—it looks like you've got yourself a roommate."

My features softened as I leaned into him. "I love you."

"I love you, too."

Epilogue

1 Year Later, November

I glanced at the clock hanging on the side wall and saw that it was twenty after four. Being that it was a Friday afternoon, I figured there was no harm letting everyone go ten minutes early. Especially because I happened to notice a special guest slip into the back of the lecture room at quarter after.

"Okay class, that's all for today," I said, my voice echoing off the walls of the large room. A murmur of excitement started amongst my students as textbooks were closed and belongings were tossed into bags. "Remember that your fourth assignment is due in the dropbox Monday afternoon, and if you have any questions, feel free to email me over the weekend or drop by my office Monday around ten for office hours. Otherwise, have a good weekend."

While most of the students left quickly, hoping for an early start to their weekend, a perky student from the front row lingered to make sure the notes she'd taken from today's lecture on the electrical function of the central nervous system were correct. And I gladly took the time to help, because she reminded me of myself at that age. Only a few months into university, and already so keen to learn as much as she could.

"These look good to me," I said after skimming over the diagrams and notes that were in her notebook. "But if you need an extra resource, everything in today's lecture is covered more in depth in chapter six of the textbook."

"Thanks," the student said, tucking her notebook into her back-pack and smiling shyly. With no one left in the room except us two and the man at the back of the class, she flitted her glaze between me and him. "Have a good weekend Professor."

My lips quirked upward, and I felt a tinge of a blush dust my cheeks. "You too."

As she turned and walked up the stairs of the lecture hall, she waved at Derrick, wishing him luck on his game tonight before scurrying out of the room.

It was strangely well-known across campus, or at least the engineering department, that I was dating one of the star forwards of the Los Angeles Royals. We'd been photographed together on a few occasions over the last year and a half, and while no one ever pestered me about it, I always heard the whispers with each term when I got a new slew of students.

Essentially, I was the cool professor.

And, if that motivated students to study and work hard in my classes, I couldn't complain.

"Well hello there," Derrick said with a silly grin, coming down to the front of the room to wrap his arms around my waist.

It wasn't often we got to see each other during the season, but he was in Boston for the night and set to face off against the Knights in less than three hours, which gave us some extra quality time together.

"Hey," I replied, extending onto my tiptoes to brush my lips softly against his. "How was your flight?"

"Fine." He shrugged. "It's always tiring flying coast to coast, especially on a plane packed with athletes, but knowing you were waiting for me was definitely a bonus."

I hummed appreciatively. "Always the charmer."

"You know it." There was a gleam in his eyes as he lifted a hand and tucked my hair behind my ear. "So, I have some news for you."

"What news?" I asked, a crease forming between my brows for a moment before my eyes widened in realization. "Oh my god, did they extend your contract?"

He nodded, joy flooding his expression, and I jumped up in celebration. I wrapped my arms tightly around his shoulders, peppering kisses on his lips.

A deep chuckle escaped him. "And that's not all," he said. "They also agreed to a no-trade clause, so while I could still technically be traded, I'd have to at least consent to it beforehand and be a part of the conversations."

"That's great!" I exclaimed. "I know you and Ken were really fighting for that."

"Yeah," he agreed. "They were actually pretty open to discussing it, which surprised me, but I think after last year the front office is seeing the value of keeping me around long-term."

After getting knocked out in the first round of the playoffs two seasons back, the Royals had come back stronger and hungrier, making it all the way to the conference finals earlier this year. Unfortunately, they'd come up short against Colorado, who'd gone on to win the Stanley Cup.

But now they were a little over a month into the new season, and having only lost one game so far, the team was once again hopeful for a long playoff run come the spring.

"Of course they want to keep you around—you were their top goal scorer last year, Mr. Hotshot. They'd be crazy to let you go." With my own news on the tip of my tongue, my excitement dimmed slightly, mixing with nerves. "Which, you know, is a good thing all things considered."

He quirked a brow. "What do you mean?"

"Well," I drawled, suddenly questioning whether I'd made the right decision not letting him in on my secret earlier, "you know how much this past off-season made us realize how much living apart has sucked?"

"Yeah..."

"What would you say if I told you I submitted an application for a research position opening up next summer in the bioengineering department at UCLA?"

Surprise overtook his features; his jaw dropping slightly and his eyes widening. "You're looking to move out to Los Angeles?"

"I mean, nothing's finalized, but someone on the faculty out there is retiring in April," I said, shifting from foot to foot. "I had a preliminary interview last week and the department head seemed to be impressed by the work I've done here. Hopefully I'll know more in the coming months, but yeah, things look promising."

"You're serious?" he asked slowly, as if my explanation wasn't enough for things to sink in. "You're coming to Los Angeles?"

I chewed on my bottom lip and nodded. "If everything works out, yeah."

We'd known each other for nearly two years now and had been together for most of that time. I knew Derrick was the one for me, and if his job had him living on the west coast for the majority of the year, I was willing to try and find a solution on my end.

Especially after finding a small, velvet box hidden in his apartment when I'd visited him a month prior.

I hadn't told him what I'd seen, but he was clearly in this relationship for the long haul, and so was I.

His elation began to shine through, though not fully, as he tightened his grip on my hips. "Are you sure though? You know I'd never ask you to—"

I silenced him with a kiss. "This isn't a choice I'm making for you," I said softly, pulling back and meeting his gaze. "I'm doing this for me, and for us. I love you, and while we've been making things work long-distance, I don't want to be doing it forever. If I can get this job, then it not only brings me to you, but it brings me closer to my family too."

"You're amazing, you know that?"

I smiled. "I've been told so once or twice."

His hands came up to cup my cheeks. "I'm serious. I love you so much."

"I love you, too."

He bent down to capture my lips with his own, kissing me thoroughly and making my heart beat faster. It was insane to me that the chemistry between us hadn't dimmed since that first night between us on New Year's Eve; it had only grown. With each kiss, each day, each moment we spent together.

And I could only see our relationship continuing on the upward trend.

After all, our future was bright, and it was just getting started.

www.ingramcontent.com/pod-product-compliance
Lightning Source LLC
Chambersburg PA
CBHW071751190726
48292CB00003B/937